ALSO BY LAURENCE KLAVAN

The Cutting Room

THE SHOOTING SCRIPT

LAURENCE KLAVAN

the SHOOTING SCRIPT

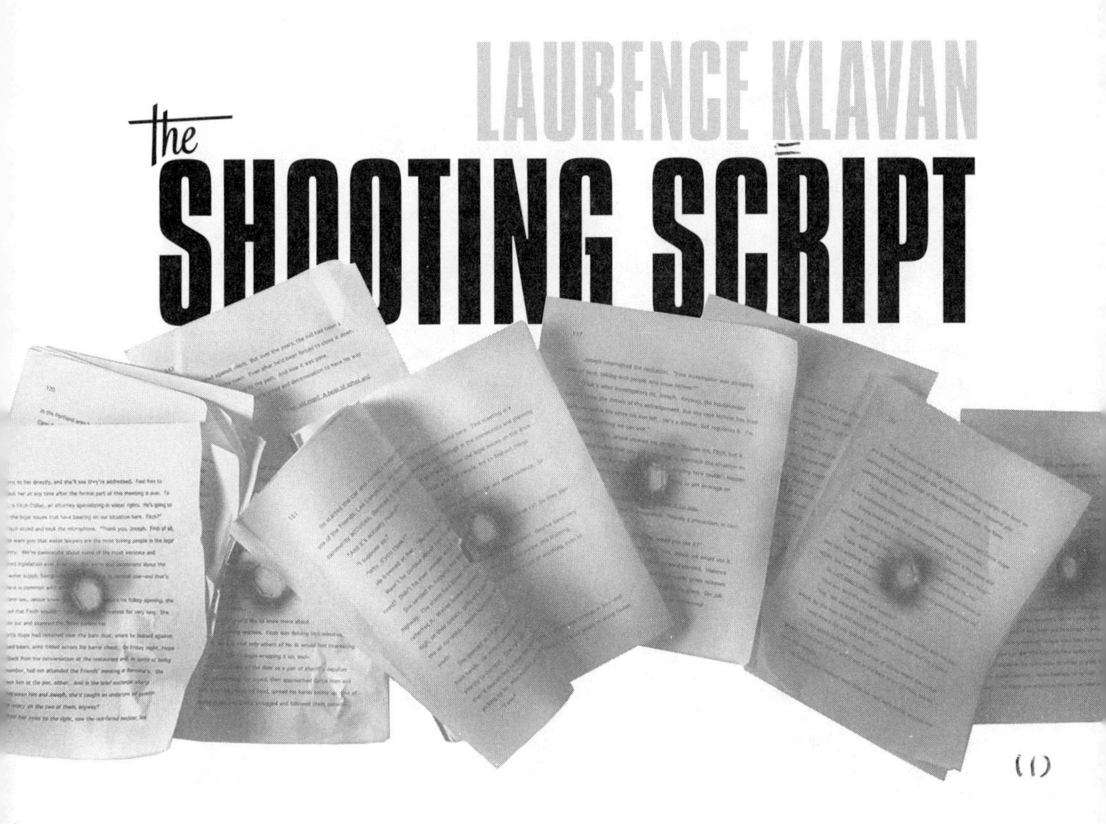

BALLANTINE BOOKS / NEW YORK

While set in real places, this book is a work of fiction. The characters and events are products of the author's imagination and should not be construed as real. Any resemblance to actual people is unintentional. In the few instances where well-known or real names are used, the related characters, incidents, or dialogues are entirely fictional and are not intended to depict any actual people or events.

A Ballantine Book
Published by The Random House Publishing Group

www.ballantinebooks.com

Library of Congress Cataloging-in-Publication Data is available from the publisher upon request.

ISBN 0-345-46276-9

Printed in the United States of America

First Edition: March 2005

9 8 7 6 5 4 3 2 1

Book design by Casey Hampton

For my mother

And in memory of my father,
who always got the joke

Dying is easy. Comedy is hard.

—attributed to the actor Edmund Gwenn, on his deathbed

PROLOGUE

THE OSCAR FOR BEST SUPPORTING ACTRESS CAME DOWN ON MY HEAD.

Before I blacked out, I saw the face of the most famous child star of the 1970s. Today, she looked like a combination of Bette Davis in *Baby Jane,* a Bel Air trophy wife, and a dead dog.

Gratey McBride stood at the top of a staircase I was ascending. She'd emerged from the shadows of the house's second floor like a bat flying from an attic. She'd even given a little batlike scream. Or maybe *I* had screamed, as she lifted then brought down the statuette she'd won for acting thirty years before.

Gratey, of course, had played an adorably cynical six-year-old grifter in the 1976 hit *Macaroon Heart*. Though it was rumored that her part had been dubbed by a male dwarf, she had still managed to nab an Oscar and a few more roles. Puberty ended her career, and adulthood brought her a tumultuous marriage, drug abuse, and oblivion.

To be honest, I wasn't that surprised to see her. I'd seen all kinds of familiar, famous, and infamous faces since I'd arrived in L.A., looking for the world's second-most coveted lost film. I, Roy Milano, had once again gone from being a passive movie sleuth to an active movie *sleuth.*

My head twanging, I felt my feet sliding out behind me, off the step, one away from the top. I fell backward as Gratey's famous, destroyed face receded into the darkness like a Halloween mask.

As I plunged down the length of the long staircase, I thought, Hey! I've never seen a real Oscar before. I'm not kidding; that's what I thought.

I better rewind this tape to the FBI Warning, right?

PART 1
NEW YORK CITY

SEQUELS ARE AS OLD AS MOVIES THEMSELVES, IF YOU COUNT A SERIAL LIKE The Perils of Pauline. The first sequel to win the Best Picture Oscar, though, was *The Godfather Part II* in 1974. The first one to be nominated in that category was probably *The Bells of St. Mary's* in 1945, the sequel to *Going My Way,* which won the year before. Bing Crosby repeated his role as . . .

Sorry. Occupational hazard.

A year ago, I had discovered the *most* sought-after "lost" film, the full version of Orson Welles's *The Magnificent Ambersons.* I thought I would like being a movie detective. After all, it beat just being what I was: a "trivial man," a person devoted to finding, hoarding, and recounting arcane movie information—in other words, a loser, I think it's generally called.

Word of my discovery had spread through the "trivial" community like a virus that caused self-loathing. From obscure fan Web sites to tiny film festivals to dusty memorabilia stores, it was rumored that I had found, then given up—without even seeing!—*Ambersons.* In the trivial world, which is populated by people even less socialized than I, the rumor led to incredulity, awe, and (of course) jealousy and hatred.

My little newsletter, *Trivial Man,* which I publish out of my jammed apartment on West Forty-third Street in New York and subsidize through typesetting work, suddenly exploded in popularity, which meant it actually sold a few copies. I began to receive phone calls from trivial people seeking my deductive services, people not accustomed to navigating in the real world.

"I've got a movie I want you to find," they'd say.

"For how much?" I'd ask, now priding myself as a professional.

Then there'd be a pause, and then I'd hear a dial tone.

I already had something over many of my colleagues: I was presentable—imagine Zeppo Marx crossed with John Garfield—had even, amazingly, been married, and still stayed in contact with my ex-wife, Jody. If you can't deal with the present, you can always depend on the past. In our own ways, Jody and I both knew this.

It was during one of Jody's usual phone calls—to ask me who was playing whom in an old movie we both, by chance, happened to be watching—that the whole thing began.

"You mean, the bandit?" I asked, muting the volume. "Akim Tamiroff." Then Call Waiting, a recent upgrade to my phone system, clicked in. "Hold on. Hello?"

There was a pause. I heard a voice I recognized. It was old, and it was downbeat.

"Roy? It's about your mother."

I don't mention my parents too often, and for good reason. Neither has the faintest idea what I'm doing with my life. Make that singular: my mother doesn't, my father's dead. But before he died, he didn't have a clue about it, either.

It always surprised me about my mother, because she loved movies, so I'd assumed my obsession had some genetic basis. (My father, who worked in insurance, never liked to leave the house for any reason, let alone movies. His usual review after seeing one consisted of three words: "Piece of crap.") My mother, however, persisted in hoping that my vast store of trivial information could lead to gainful employment, marriage, and DNA propagation. No such luck.

"What do you do with a thing like that?" she'd usually ask after I'd made the mistake of sharing some little-known fact with her, like, for instance that Maggie Smith had replaced Katharine Hepburn in *Travels with My Aunt*. "Why don't you write your own column?"

"I put out my own newsletter," I'd reply. "I sort of do that already."

"No, I mean, you know, for real."

I assumed she'd be encouraged by my discovery of the complete *Ambersons,* and the idea of dealing with her ("What do you do with a thing like that? Why don't you join the FBI?") caused me to stay mum.

Now Mom was the one who was mum.

Apparently she—as my aunt informed me on the phone—was no longer speaking. There seemed no physical problem; it was apparently a head thing. It wasn't unprecedented—once, my mother had hidden under the kitchen table all afternoon; another time she'd been found wandering the neighborhood in her nightgown—but this event, or so my aunt believed, was a keeper. No amount of medication mattered. My mother was no longer a moving picture; she was a still.

"But what do you want *me* to do?" I asked Aunt Ruby, as I followed her down the stairs. I hadn't been in the old family house in the Westchester suburbs since Thanksgiving; now it was March.

"Help pay for the upkeep," said my aunt. She was a frighteningly practical and direct woman, a registered nurse, and my mother's only other relation. She referred to her kid sister as if she were no different from the familiar, crumbling home we were in. That was life to Ruby: we all just became a question of maintenance.

"Well . . . for how long?"

"For as long as it takes."

"But—" I stammered lamely, "she's only seventy. She could live another twenty years."

My mother was no vegetable. Lying silently in bed, she still showed a hearty appetite and flicked efficiently through TV stations. Her eyes had even sparkled a little when I walked in. Still, none of my small talk had brought a response.

"Twenty years or even twenty-five," Aunt Ruby agreed, unhelpfully.

"Well, she's got health insurance—Medicare—doesn't she?"

"These days you can never have enough."

This was true. I myself at thirty-six—the time everything "starts to go," my aunt once remarked—was uncovered. I was running out of reasons to resist. "But things are just starting to pick up for me."

"Good. Then it shouldn't be a problem."

I stopped at the front door. "You have no idea what might have caused her to become like this?"

My aunt only shrugged. "Something must have rubbed her the wrong way."

For Aunt Ruby, the comment summed up diseases, accidents, even death itself. It made a funny kind of sense, yet I had to keep fighting this lost cause.

"Look, let me know if she says anything, okay?"

"Don't worry, Roy. You'll be the first to know." It was the only time I had ever heard Aunt Ruby laugh.

I had no siblings, so I had no choice.

As usual, remembering trivia was my way to deal with anxiety. Standing outside the house, I remembered that the original stars of *Sons and Lovers* were supposed to be Alec Guinness and Montgomery Clift. The film was finally made with Trevor Howard and Dean Stockwell.

The picture had been nominated for the Oscar; my fate would be less prestigious. Just as I was on the verge of a new career in detection, I had to do something that I'd never done before, something truly frightening. I had to get a real job.

A WEEK LATER, I WAS STANDING ON THE STREET, HOLDING A BAGUETTE AND a balloon.

Trivial people take all kinds of part-time, low-paying jobs, some more humiliating than others. Through contacts, I'd managed to secure employment at the Farmer's Market in Union Square. Here, upstate farmers sold produce to gullible urbanites willing to shell out exorbitantly for organic goods. A friend who'd been laid off from a film journal had been helping out at several stands and tipped me off to similar opportunities. I could do pickles, pretzels, or bread. The latter was a staple and so seemed the least demeaning.

"U-shin sent me," I'd said, mentioning my friend.

Annabelle, the young lady farmer at the Nature's Meal booth, had a pretty face the color and texture of a leather belt. She looked at my pale skin and slender frame with amusement.

"Okay, pavement boy," she said. "Here you go."

Then she handed me the balloon and the loaf. She pinned a button on my chest that read RISING BREAD, FALLING PRICES! Her bakery, located in Millwood, two hours from Manhattan, was having a sale.

"Just stand there," she said, in a gruff and grizzled rasp. "And look pretty." Then she shook her head in dismay, as she might have at a newborn calf too weak to survive.

I was secretly hoping that my city ways and her country manner would cause romantic sparks, as in a Tracy and Hepburn film. But Annabelle quickly moved away from me and arranged some zucchini and pear muffins.

As I stood there, mortified, I recalled that Spencer Tracy had been replaced by Gregory Peck in the movie of *The Yearling*. The whole film had been remade from scratch, just like, well, a burnt loaf.

Then, to my horror, I saw Abner Cooley.

Abner, of course, was the original trivial person success story. His Web site, PRINTIT!.com, had grown from a homemade operation—done, literally, out of his parents' house on Long Island—into a grassroots phenomenon. It mostly featured negative gossip on forthcoming films secretly slipped to him by bitter studio underlings. Frightened and annoyed executives had seduced Abner with consulting jobs, and then he'd parlayed his popularity into a book deal and a TV hosting gig. The latter came courtesy of his boyfriend, Taylor Weinrod, recently promoted to V.P. at Landers Classic Movies, or LCM, the old movie cable network.

As his success had—you'll pardon me—ballooned, so had Abner. Never a sylph, he now threatened to topple over from his own girth, and a wispy blond beard, as ever, couldn't give shape to his face. Formerly obnoxious, he was now unbearable, and never more so than today, when he saw me . . . and my balloon.

"Milano!" he said, with barely disguised glee. "What a pleasant surprise!"

Abner had never forgiven me for my *Ambersons* coup, and seeing me in my current position clearly warmed his overgrown heart.

"I'm sure it is," I said.

"A loaf of bread, a red balloon . . . you could be the star of, what was that French film?"

"*The Red Balloon*?" I asked.

"Yes," he said, unpleasantly. "So, fallen on hard times?"

"I'm just helping out a friend," I lied.

Just then, Annabelle called over, "Hey, what's-your-name, watch your loaf! It's trailing in the dirt!"

Exposed, I cursed under my breath and said nothing more. Abner chuckled, his cheeks expanding, his eyes disappearing.

"How generous of you," he said.

I could have told him the truth—Abner would be chastened by my helping out my mother; God knows he'd lived long enough with his own—but I didn't want to give him the satisfaction. So I didn't take the bait.

"Well, I'm sure you'll get back on your feet in no time. Now," he said, mischievously, "may I have some *miche*?"

"You'll have to ask *her,*" I said, through my teeth, and gestured with my balloon at Annabelle.

"Actually, what am I saying? It'll only go bad in my fridge. I'm flying out to L.A. tomorrow."

"Bon voyage."

Though I hadn't asked him why, he went on to explain. "Maybe you read the trades. I've been hired to adapt *The Seven Ordeals of Quelman*."

My only response was silence. Here was the most famous and beloved cult fantasy novel—four sets of trilogies, actually—of all time. And Abner Cooley had been hired to write the script! I had never been able to finish the first book. I had no interest in, intention of, or talent at being a screenwriter. Still, I was boiling with anger at the injustice.

"Good for you," I choked out.

"Yep. They decided to go right to the source for once. The producers want a few changes that might not sit well with the fans in geekville. But"—he shrugged, cavalierly—"that's the difference between film and book."

Film and *book*! Abner wasn't even using the proper plurals; he was talking like one of the studio scum he had started his career by skewering. He had fully completed his duplicitous journey to the other side, where people made a living wage. And *geekville*? Where did Abner think he got his *own* birth certificate?

"Good luck with that," I nearly whispered.

"Thanks. It'll be twelve films in all. They'll release the first one next Christmas, then three a year until the end of the decade."

"Can't wait."

Abner heard the sarcasm in my voice and, if anything, it made him even more smug. "Look . . . there's nothing wrong with doing what you're doing. We all need to eat."

"Some more than others," I blurted out. I knew the remark was beneath me, but I didn't care. I realized that I was gripping the baguette—onion sourdough, I think—like a club.

"Hey, street life!" Annabelle yelled over at me now. "Quit flirting, and make that sale!"

The furious look in my eye made Abner cancel his order. With a muttered, "Good to see you, Milano," he walked away as fast as his giant legs could take him.

There was a brief, embarrassing pause. Then Annabelle, smelling of bread dust and denim, was suddenly at my side again.

"That's not exactly what I'd call good salesmanship," she said.

"Look," I answered, just about at patience's end, "I thought I was only supposed to look pretty."

"Oh," Annabelle said, "I say that to all the girls."

Then, with a sunburned little smile, she walked behind her booth again.

I stared after her. Despite her disdain for me, in her cruel, craggy, cowgirl way, Annabelle was growing more attractive by the minute. I noted with approval how she filled out her jeans. This job might not be so bad, after all.

When I turned back, I was staring at Abner's big face again.

"Look, Milano," he said, breathless now. "How'd you like to come work for *me*?"

The twist of personality had come so fast, I shook my head to clear it. "What?"

"There's something I forgot to tell you."

"And what's that?"

"Someone," he panted, "is trying to kill me."

ON A BREAK—FOR WHICH I HAD TO BEG ANNABELLE—I HEARD ABNER'S story.

We sat in a diner on Park Avenue South at Seventeenth Street, which was cheaper than anything he could now afford. And even though Abner spoke with a new beseeching neediness, he still insisted on separate checks.

Before he started, he looked around for eavesdroppers. "Here's the thing. The *Quelman* gig isn't exactly the joyride I'd been expecting."

I listened with reluctant sympathy. My tolerance for Abner was already limited and today he was adding a new unpleasant color to his palette: self-pity. Still, it *was* new.

"You know Prince Corno?" he asked.

"Who?"

"Prince Corno, from the first three volumes?"

I vaguely had some memory of a character named this from my brief time spent skimming the *Quelman* fantasies. "What about him?"

"Remember that he's called 'The Great Lonely One'?"

I shrugged. "Sure."

"Well, that's not how the suits in Cali want him to remain."

I cringed at Abner's new jargon. "Speak English."

"Corno's a warrior. A leader of men. His only companion is his little omniscient owl, Shaba. Generations of readers know this and love him for it. And the executives want—get this—for him to have a girlfriend."

I broke off a piece of my bagel, waiting for Abner to get to the point.

"And not just any girlfriend. They want him to get it on with Lady Baluga. Queen of the Second Peninsula? They want me to add a love story between Prince Corno and Lady Baluga!"

Abner was so distressed that he was hardly touching his butter-slathered pancakes. Then he pushed the plate away altogether.

"Hey," I said, torturing him, "you signed on for this. That's the outside world."

"I don't—" he checked around again, lowering his voice. "I don't blame them. They've made a huge investment, and they need everyone on earth to show up. Canoodling between Corno and Baluga will add more of the fifteen- to thirty-five-year-old-female demographic, which is the only sector that's lagging in their focus group testing. I understand that."

I knew what he meant, but hassled him again anyway. "It's like you're speaking in a foreign tongue."

"In other words, Milano, it wouldn't be that big an issue. Except that . . . it's gotten out. And the information's fallen into the worst possible hands."

I nodded, slowly perceiving where he was going.

"You mean . . ."

"Exactly. The fans. Someone working in the movie studio—some secretary, some nobody!—leaked the information to the fan Web sites. Now it's all over the Net. And so is my face!"

His wide hands shaking, Abner slowly unfolded a printout from his pocket. It had been reproduced from a Web site called Quelman House: All Things Quelman. There was a fuzzy photo of Abner, with the word *traitor* stamped on it. The article below featured the headlines: COOLEY UNCOOL, SAY NO TO HOLLYWOOD DESECRATION, and, in smaller print, HE SHOULD ONLY HAVE AN OWL.

I couldn't help but smile at the irony. Now *Abner* represented Hollywood venality; he had been betrayed by the very underlings on whom he had once depended. But the bigger man's obvious, sincere dismay was starting to work on my sympathies.

"I wouldn't have minded just the threatening phone calls or the harassing e-mails . . ." He unsteadily opened another sheet. It was an electronic missive that started, "Eat *this,* you fat, betraying sack of . . ." and Abner's elbow obscured the rest.

"I mean, that's a healthy debate," he chuckled, uneasily. "But . . . the other thing is really freaking me out."

To my shock, Abner started to undress. I wondered if his discombobulation had officially unbalanced him. He unbuttoned his collarless, Seventies-style shirt, and exposed a vast pink-and-blond chest. He also revealed something else: two small and encrusted stab wounds.

"Look," he said. "This is what I'm talking about."

"Jesus." I didn't know what was harder to witness: Abner's flesh or his flesh wounds. Either way, getting the point, I gestured for him to cover up.

After he had, he continued. "It wasn't the first time he came at me, but it *was* the first time he got me."

"He? Who do you mean?"

"This guy, this fanatic. He's followed me down the street. He's chased me in a car. One night, he waited for me, in the lobby of our building. That's when he did this—with an X-Acto blade. 'This is for Corno, you bastard!' he screamed, as the knife went in. 'And *this* is for Baluga!' I had to run. From my own house! When I got back from the hospital, he was gone. Lucky for me the blade didn't go in too deep."

I nodded. "What did the cops say?"

"The cops?" Here Abner looked surprised. "What do you think? While they laughed, I made out a report."

I was almost touched. I knew what it was like to try and get help from a cop. For all his newfound success and arrogance, Abner was still, in the eyes of the authorities, a worthless misfit. Whether aspiring screenwriter or sleuth, we would both always be reminded of who we really were.

"That's why I'm talking to *you,* Milano."

"Really?"

"How'd you like to come work for me? Find this guy. That's what you do least badly, isn't it? Find things?"

I slowly swallowed a chunk of my bagel. It was the closest Abner could come to a compliment. Since I'd found *Ambersons,* his respect for me had obviously grown. Especially if he could make use of my services.

"It's an interesting proposition" was all I said. "But how much are we talking about?"

Abner told me. In the scheme of things, it was a weak offer; he was still a cheap louse. But compared to what I was getting for working with a balloon, it was a ransom. However, I didn't reply.

Snooping for Abner was an indignity I could never have imagined. But more money would mean more help for my mother. And this job was *sort of* in the new profession that I wished to pursue. I just hoped Annabelle the farmer would understand.

I held out until Abner upped the price a bit. Then I shook his hand, wet from syrup and sweat. We agreed that I would start immediately.

I started sooner than that. Just then, a bullet hit the window.

A REAL BULLET WOULD HAVE SHATTERED THE GLASS. AT LEAST THAT'S WHAT I assumed from all the movies I'd seen. This projectile just made a deafening sound and formed its own sunburst. It loomed right over Abner's head, giving him a halo that was anything but innocent.

I only knew one thing. The shot had come from inside the restaurant.

As Abner hit the dirt, literally scrambling beneath the booth table, I whirled around. The few others eating in the dingy diner were also staring, hiding, or, in the case of one old gal, calmly turning a page of a newspaper.

One man was running out the door.

He was wiry and in his thirties. His face was covered by a ski mask, his body by a peacoat too heavy for the day.

Within a second, I was after him. I didn't even think. This was my job again, wasn't it?

When I got out to Park Avenue, I saw the shooter heading south. I realized two things: I wasn't wearing a jacket, and I was scared. A mix of chill and raging sweat gave me this information. As I took a deep breath and began to pump toward him, I remembered that Tyrone Power had died of a heart attack on the set of *Solomon and Sheba*. The producers had replaced him with Yul Brynner.

The guy was pushing people out of the way, though no more brusquely than someone late for work. The worst he got were dirty looks. Running against lights, dodging cars, he reached Fifteenth Street, on which he took a shrieking left, going east. I had drifted a street and a half behind. What kind of obsessed geek was in such good shape? I wondered.

Hanging the turn at a slower pace, I saw him farther down Fifteenth, on his way to Irving Place. He was fast approaching a mini–theater row of off-Broadway houses. He glanced around once and, for a second, I caught his eyes, which were circled by the mask. Then I looked at the pocket of his coat, which I assumed held the pellet or beebee, but still dangerous, weapon he had used.

Turning forward again, he nearly smashed into a theater crew, which was loading in a show. Blocking the street, they lugged cables, props, and furniture. After skidding to a halt, he disappeared into their midst, then was covered by a scrim of gray sky being carried by a grip. When the clouds parted, he was gone. The door to the theater stood open.

Reaching the theater crew, I did more than he had done: I gave a heartfelt apology. Then, weaving through them, I ran inside the theater, too.

Within the small lobby, I caught a glimpse of the ski mask as it disappeared down a central stairs. I saw him reach a floor below and dart inside the theater space, the doors of which hung open. Panting, my legs throbbing, I followed him, breaking into the theater with a helpless gasp.

I thought: Bette Davis had replaced Claudette Colbert in *All About Eve,* after the latter hurt her back.

Onstage, more people from the crew were hanging lights and hoisting flats. The theater held about one hundred and fifty seats. In a center row, the man in the ski mask was moving toward the farther side.

When I looked where he was heading, I saw a ramp that led, I would have bet, downstairs.

I descended another tiny set of steps and cut into the row. As I did, the man turned around once, then moved faster. We couldn't help but attract attention from those onstage.

"Hey!" somebody shouted. "What, are they shooting something?"

"What is it, *Law and Order*?"

"You can't do that in here!"

"We've got the space!"

Then the scene they witnessed became more real. I hurtled out my hand and grabbed the collar of the other man's coat. Once he was in my grip, I pulled him backward, harshly, toward me. With a grunt, he twirled around and punched me in the shoulder, shocking me with pain and knocking me off-balance. I released my grip and slipped onto a closed seat, which flapped open, but not soon enough to catch me.

"What the hell's going on?" I heard from the stage, as I hit the floor.

Only taking a second to be stunned, I turned, flung out both hands, and grabbed hold of the escaping man's ankles. Now it was his turn to be decked, and he fell forward in the space between the rows.

"Knock it off!" one stagehand yelled.

"Call the cops!"

"Free show!"

I tried dragging my target back by his feet. But both of his boots kicked out at me, and only a fast yank sideways saved my face from being smashed. Surprisingly undaunted, I sprang upon his back, as if I were leaping on a surfboard. I pressed him to the dirty floor, as his hands sprang back and clawed at me.

"Please stop," I said, exhausted.

I heard people start to scramble from the stage, drawn by the sounds of combat behind the seats. Meanwhile, the man beneath me suddenly brought his head up and back. I caught a whiff of linty, unwashed cotton as his masked skull came a half-inch from colliding with my nose.

Leaning back to avoid it, I lost my dominance, and he took full advantage. Flinging out his arms, he shucked me like a bronc shedding its rider. I landed faceup on the floor, and he scrambled to his feet.

The shock of my descent made me immobile. I heard the man peeling from the aisle, making it to the ramp. As he escaped out that side, the stagehands reached me from the other end. I looked up, saw them above me, still burly, upside down.

"You all right?" one asked.

"I don't know," I answered, and it was true.

"Who *is* that guy?"

"He tried to rob me."

"Should we call the cops?"

I shook my head. "What's down that ramp?"

"Dressing rooms," one answered.

In another minute, I had hobbled down the ramp myself. My legs ached as if they'd been burned by smokes. My head felt twice its size from smacking the theater floor. And my lower back—I have no words to express the agony.

Slowly easing down yet another staircase, I found myself in a small hall of uninhabited dressing rooms. A cool wind directed my attention to the hall's end, where an Exit door stood conspicuously open. Then I stopped at and entered a dressing room.

I looked at myself in the mirror, which was ringed by white Broadway bulbs. All told, I looked okay. Most of my wounds were invisible. Still, I thought my hairline might be receding.

When I turned to the left, I saw a rack of costumes, apparently uncollected from an earlier show. There was a feather boa, a man's Navy dress uniform, and a fake fur coat. There was also, on the floor beneath it, hastily discarded like the disguises they were, a ski mask and a peacoat.

Outside the diner, police crime tape now barred the door, a sign on which read CLOSED. No cops, however, were in sight.

I stood at the door, and waved through its glass at the owner. The only one inside, he was an Indian-American guy, sitting at a booth, his head drooped, forlornly. He rose and unlocked the place.

"I'm the guy who chased him," I said.

"You're the one," he sighed. "A waiter told me. I got something for you."

He let me in. Then he walked to the counter, reached behind, and pulled out an envelope. This he placed in my hands.

"A fat guy left it for you."

I nodded. Inside, folded neatly, was a check holding a Post-it. Abner had scrawled on it, *Your first installment,* and he had paid what we agreed. He had, of course, forgotten to sign it, but that wasn't a surprise.

"Anybody get a look at the other guy's face?" I asked. "The shooter?"

He shook his head. "He kept the mask on, ordered a coffee, then did his thing."

There were other, heavier objects at the bottom of the envelope. I shook them out upon the counter.

"That's what he left," the owner said. "His tip."

There were three dimes.

"You didn't give these to the cops?" I asked.

The owner shrugged. "You cared more."

I smiled. Carefully, I scooped the coins—worth more at that moment than the check—into my pocket.

Then, from behind the counter, the owner brought me a plate, wrapped in plastic. He uncovered what was left of my bagel.

"Want me to heat it up?"

"No, thanks."

It tasted great just the way it was.

ANNABELLE THE FARMER LET ME GO WITH A SOFT—AFFECTIONATE, I hoped?—cry of "Traitor!" Then she pressed a Nature's Meal card in my front shirt pocket and wrapped a plastic bag filled with sour rye around my wrist. Her sturdy, almost painful hold of my neck afterward was arousing, though I would never tell a soul.

I had no time to lose.

If Abner was in such jeopardy that he was nearly killed during brunch, the situation was as serious as he said. Luckily, I had my suspicions about who could help.

The next day, I leafed through an illustrated edition of the entire *Seven Ordeals of Quelman,* which was too heavy for me to hold. My bruised arms straining beneath its weight, I placed it on a table at Dynomics, the comic book store, which was the first place I'd hit.

The dusty collector's haven was in Williamsburg, Brooklyn, about half a mile from the Brooklyn-Queens Expressway underpass. It used to be on Fourteenth Street between Seventh and Eighth in Manhattan, but that space was now a new and shiny chain pharmacy. Times change.

"Be careful with that."

I looked up and saw Jeff Losson, the store's owner, peering at me from an aisle stacked with *Supermans*. He was a lean, ageless hippie type—probably around thirty-seven—with long hair tied in a ponytail and cold eyes covered by small round glasses. He always spoke in a snide whisper and his snickering laugh betrayed as much self-loathing as amusement.

"Unless you got five hundred bucks," he added.

With an effort, I closed the massive tome. "I'm not a big fan."

"You'd have to know how to read, Roy. Not just watch."

As a comic book/fantasy novel expert, Losson looked down on mere movies. He only featured one meager row on the subject in his store. We knew each other mildly, and usually kept our distance. But I was aware that he edited the online fan site Quelman House.

"I bet you'll be first in line when the movie comes out," I said. "The *movies,* I mean."

"Yeah, right." Losson snickered. Then, as usual, he segued into a miserable sigh, admitting I was right. "But at least I'll hiss Abner Cooley's name."

"That's better than trying to kill him."

Losson snorted. "I heard he's been having trouble. Maybe he should think twice about adding the love story."

"Don't act so innocent. You pretty much put a price on his head on your site."

"Give me a break."

"You at least contributed to a violent atmosphere."

"It was all in good fun." Then he stared at me through his tinted lenses. "Since when do *you* care about Abner?"

"I don't. It just seems a bit extreme, that's all."

Losson shrugged, still confused about my interest. At all costs, I wished to avoid admitting that I worked for Abner; it was too embarrassing. But how much longer could I keep it secret?

Losson was no dummy. His eyes grew wide. "What!" he blurted out. "You're Cooley's coolie now? The fat man's bitch?"

Cursing, silently, I felt myself blush. Then I turned away. "I got a sick mother."

Losson gave a full-fledged whinnying laugh. Then it melted into one more unhappy moan, before he wondered, "Who doesn't?"

I turned back, slowly, sensing a connection neither one of us wanted to explore. But its existence allowed me to be direct. "You know who's hounding him?"

Losson's slight shoulders went up and down. "Beats me. But no jury would convict."

It was my turn to sigh. "Yeah, I guess. Well, thanks a lot. For nothing."

The conversation—and the bonding—was over. It was as far as two hard-boiled nerds could go. Still, the store was empty but for me. So I brought a used Robert Mitchum biography to the counter. I remembered that Peter O'Toole had replaced him in Otto Preminger's disaster *Rosebud.*

I flipped out bills. After I had counted out change, he pushed some coins back at me. "Nice try."

"What do you mean?"

When I looked down, I saw the three dimes I'd gotten at the diner. They were supposed to be evidence; I was using them to buy a movie book. It was only my second case.

"Try that trick on someone else."

"Aren't they . . ." I picked up the dimes, checking the faces of FDR.

"All those movies have ruined your retinas. Can't you see they're play money?"

"They are?" I stared, mortified, at the worthless faux-silver. "Well, I'm not a Treasury agent," I said, abashed. "They were left behind by Abner's stalker."

The information just fell out of me, to divert Losson from my ineptitude. It had a different effect.

Losson moved back a bit, as if from a hideous smell. He paused, as if deciding whether to reveal something. Then he skipped his snicker and went right to his sigh that meant, what do I care? I'm crap.

"Look," he said. "It must be Stanley Lager."

I stared at him, shocked. "*What?*"

Stanley Lager was a trivial man I hadn't heard of in a while. He was an amoral borderline nut who skipped from one expertise to another. In recent years it was said he'd fallen into dissolution, using drugs, altering himself with plastic surgery, living off of male and female lovers. He now just used trivia opportunistically, culling and selling collectibles online. The rest of us prided ourselves on *knowing* things; we lived through it, not *off* it; what Stanley did was a desecration.

In truth, he frightened us. Stanley Lager was, we secretly felt, our dark, unstable side. But trying to kill Abner over a fantasy novel?

"Can that really be true?" I asked.

Losson shrugged. "I've heard Stanley's hiding from someone he ripped off. He's been living in a maid's room in an old, upstate mansion. One of those big-ass houses near West Point, used to be owned by the Roosevelts, or somebody. Now it's open to the public. Turns out, despite tourism, the joint is crumbling and getting broken into a lot, so they took in a border. Those fake dimes are the souvenirs they hand out at the tour."

I nodded. "Jesus."

"It's in Millwood, I think."

The town rang a bell. It was near Rhinebeck, the site of a fan film festival, in which *Ambersons* had figured. I suddenly remembered a whiff of sour rye; it was also where Annabelle's bakery was. It took me a second to snap out of the romantic reverie.

"Thanks, Losson," I said, sincerely.

"Sure, Roy. But, if you see Stanley, be careful. He's . . ." Losson circled the side of his head with a finger. He snickered. Then he sighed one last time, as if to say, look who's talking.

When I got home, I was feeling pretty cocky. Even though the discovery was totally accidental, I now had a good lead on Abner's tormentor. It wasn't just a lead; I knew exactly who it must be: Stanley Lager.

An online search yielded one fuzzy photo of Stanley. It was an *LA Weekly* feature from a few years back; he was a guide on an *I Love Lucy* landmarks tour. His obscured face seemed ferrety beneath his jaunty cap. But if he liked plastic surgery, who knew how he looked today?

Then I stopped short. What an idiot I was. That meant it was the end of the case. I hadn't even negotiated a bonus or anything if I found the perpetrator. One unsigned check from Abner—how much health care for my mother was *that* going to buy?

I had no stomach for doing anything else now. I turned back to my computer, hoping to divert myself on a trivia site.

Then one e-mail made me forget everything else.

It came from an address I'd never seen before: Ted6569. It was addressed to me personally. It read:

Dear Roy,

Love your work. I've got Clown. *Let's meet.*

I CAUGHT MY BREATH. I KNEW EXACTLY WHAT IT MEANT.

My mystery correspondent was referring to *The Day the Clown Cried,* Jerry Lewis's famous uncompleted film. It was a departure for Lewis, a serious drama based on a true story about a circus clown used by the Nazis to escort children into the gas chambers. Directing and starring, Lewis had shot the film in Sweden in 1972 with a cast that also included one of Ingmar Bergman's leading ladies, Harriet Andersson.

The film was reportedly plagued by money problems and creative angst. In the end, Lewis never officially finished or released it. As the years went by, he refused to even discuss it publicly. Though rough cuts have apparently been screened for various colleagues and insiders—and the entire script featured on a guerrilla Web site—it had never been seen by any real critic or film historian, let alone the general public.

Next to *The Magnificent Ambersons,* it was the most notorious and elusive "get" in the trivial world.

My hands nearly shaking, I proceeded to answer the e-mail. I wrote back what I thought was a cool and cryptic reply, not betraying my almost head-bending need.

Dear Ted 6569:

If you mean what you say . . . [I originally wrote a hip "let's get it on," then a belligerent "let's rumble," then a wimpy] *why not?*

The reply was almost instantaneous. A meeting was arranged in two days at a flophouse hostel that called itself a hotel in Hell's Kitchen. He left a room number but no last name.

As I got offline, I reflected on the writer's probably temporary and definitely impoverished address. If he really had the film, I couldn't arrive empty-handed and come away with it. If he didn't have the film, I could be rolled the minute I walked in. Only the first possibility gave me pause.

Forget working for Abner, *this* was the kind of job I'd been waiting for. But with Abner's case solved, my access to cash would be over. No amount of typesetting or, for that matter, loaf hawking, would make it up. Now I had more than my mother to support: I again had my trivial habit, and it gnawed at me like the need for a needle.

My only option didn't make me particularly proud: stall Abner, keep collecting his checks for my own secret purposes, and run the risk of Stanley Lager attacking him once more, maybe fatally.

How much did I dislike Abner? How much did I love—or at least, feel obligated—to my mother? How much did I want to see *The Day the Clown Cried*? As a movie detective's life got more complex, so did his moral quandaries.

To my surprise, Abner made the first move.

"I never went to Cali," he said, on a scratchy, inadequately charged cell phone. "Let's take a meeting."

The meeting wasn't with Abner alone.

I showed up at the plush apartment he now shared with Taylor Weinrod, which was their "New York base," as opposed to "our L.A.

pad." Immediately, I saw a leather jacket and a suede vest slung on a coat-rack in the vestibule. As I proceeded into the living room, I heard low, satiny murmurs coming from within.

They were the voices of two men, obviously the studio suits Abner had mentioned. The moniker was misapplied today: trying to look bohemian for their East Coast trip, the executives had donned pressed jeans and Polo shirts. One wore sandals on his pedicured feet, the other had expensive lace-up sneakers. Abner sat opposite them, still intentionally or helplessly, looking big and ragged by comparison.

"Milano," he said, but didn't rise.

The men glanced up and smiled, politely, but neither shook my hand. I caught a glimpse of myself in a gold-framed mirror. In my wrinkled *On the Waterfront* T-shirt and cargo pants, I realized I must look like Abner's homeless and deranged friend. The two could enjoy the bohemian style of a kooky writer they had hired; his revolting pals were something else again.

"Take a seat," Abner went on. "I was just telling Sandy and Toby about my little, uh, situation."

I sat, uneasily. The lack of welcome filled me with dread, and I suddenly recalled that George Cukor had replaced Robert Mulligan as the director of *Rich and Famous;* it was the old director's last film.

Abner was gesturing to a sheet of paper on a glass table between them. I made out the threatening e-mail he had shown me.

"And if that isn't bad enough," he was telling them, "take a look at this . . ."

Again, Abner started to undress.

My eyes rolling, unhappily, I checked out the view from his and Taylor's Riverside Drive penthouse. As I watched boats chugging up the Hudson, I heard the uncomfortable sighs of his bosses as they were exposed to his flesh. Then, picking up sounds of a shirt being pulled back on, I returned my gaze.

"Check this out, too."

Abner had placed a few photographs on the table. They were hastily snapped shots of the bullet-grazed diner window.

"Milano here took these, as part of his investigation." Abner gave me a quick glance that warned me not to contradict. "I got his name from a friend who'd had a nasty divorce." Then he spoke to his two guests in a mano-a-mano undertone. "And I wouldn't have hired someone like *him* if things weren't this far gone. If the threats continue, I'll have no choice but to charge him to the studio."

The two execs checked out the pictures and then me, with equal distaste.

"You got anything to add before I rest my case?" Abner asked me, and his cold stare told me I did not.

Ticked off at being treated like disreputable help—and lied about, to boot—I shook my head very, very slowly.

"Good." Abner turned back to his friends. "Now I don't mean to pressure you, but if you want me to make the deadline for my first draft, somebody's got to pull the trigger about the love story . . . in a manner of speaking." He chuckled, but I could sense he was nervous.

The two execs looked thoughtfully at each other. Then one leaned in close to Abner, and his sweet cologne wafted into my nose.

"Can we speak in private?" he asked, discreetly.

"Sure," Abner answered. Then, without hesitation, he told me, "There are grapes in the kitchen."

I sat in Abner and Taylor's immaculate kitchen, looking at a mounted set of knives, debating whether to carve my initials into their fancy, Fifties-style Formica table. I had no more moral qualms. I would lie to Abner outright, tell him I had no idea who was threatening him, then mount a lengthy investigation and bleed his walrus body white. If he got killed in the meantime, that was life. I might be able to help my mother and get to see *The Day the Clown Cried*.

I heard muffled talk from the next room, then people standing up, and a back or two being slapped. Leather and suede were pulled and zipped. The front door opened and closed. Then Abner hissed out, "Yesss!"

In a second, he was spread across the kitchen doorway.

"Well," he said, smiling broadly, his face a shocking shade of pink. "Looks like that's the end of the story. The love story, I mean."

Whistling, he marched forward, his short arms swinging, like a merry squire in an operetta. He placed his fingers into a bowl of grapes and broke off an entire stem. Then he tried to fit them all into his mouth at one time.

A second later, they were stomped on the floor, and I wasn't making wine.

"What the hell are you doing?!" I screamed.

"What do you mean?" he asked, stunned, looking down at his flattened snack. "Saving the project. It worked perfectly. They'd rather eighty-six the love story than incite the whole fan base, let alone pay for *my* protection. I played them, like a—what do you call it?—a fancy violin."

Grumbling at the mess, Abner stooped to retrieve the fruit but didn't, to my surprise, put it back in his mouth.

"Then you mean—" I was stammering now. "That's *it*?"

"Look, we scratched each other's backs. You got a check. And I got a final spur to get the L.A. boys to cave. It's just lucky I went shopping for bread that day, right?"

Abner chuckled, fingering a new batch of grapes, but tentatively, assessing my mood. As I saw my meal ticket—an appropriate name for him—disappearing, I desperately grabbed onto any argument I could find.

"But . . . what about . . . the guy? The fanatic? He's still out there, you know."

Abner's answer was at the ready. "Prince Corno and Lady Beluga won't be making kissy-face anymore. So he'll have nothing to be mad about. He'll fade back into the ether. Case closed."

He was right, of course. Abner had thought of everything and with more savvy than I would ever have given him credit for. It left me out in the ether, too, or the cold, or in the dust, or wherever the worst place was. It left me with just my mother. And she might soon be gone.

I lunged across the table at him.

The two of us crashed down onto his slick, parqueted floor. We rolled into the legs of the kitchen table, toppling two of the chairs. No fighter, Abner was slapping both of his hands into my back, like he was playing a bass. Not doing much better, I was pinching his cheeks like a psychotic relative.

I remembered that Lee Remick had replaced Lana Turner in *Anatomy of a Murder*. Something about the costumes.

"Milano," Abner cringed, kneeing me continually in the thigh, "what the hell are you doing?"

The question didn't stop me; something else did. Abner had pushed a small gun into my head.

"DON'T WORRY," HE SAID. "IT ISN'T REAL."

It had done its job, however. I had stopped long enough for him to disengage from me. Then Abner found his feet and brushed off his own T-shirt, which was adorned with a blow-up of the *Variety* article about his screenplay gig.

Abner put the little gun into a drawer of the kitchen table and shut it. Panting, he told me, "Taylor keeps it around for protection. I think they're pellets. Whatever it shoots, they ain't bullets."

His stalker had a phony gun; so did Abner. Coins were fake; checks couldn't be cashed. In the world Abner moved in, the risks were phony and even death was negotiable. I alone was left in the place where things either hurt like hell or were lost forever. I didn't like it.

"Look," I said, "I might have *Clown*."

Abner looked up from his next position, his head under the faucet, cold water running on his generous neck. His move was sudden, and the water splashed all over his hair.

"What?" he said, dripping wet.

"You heard me."

I had revealed my deepest secret to my worst archrival. What else could I do? I wanted to be back in action, and a detective needs a bankroll. These days, everyone was merging; big fish ate little fish; Abner Cooley could be my—what do they call it?—corporate parent. I wasn't proud of it, but what was I *ever* proud of? This was what I told myself.

I had taken a risk, too. Maybe Abner had gone so far Hollywood that such a trivial pursuit no longer interested him. Yet, when I saw him staring, oblivious to the water that flooded his face, hair, and shirt, I knew that he still had needs more irrational than money or fame.

"Tell me," he whispered.

After I did, Abner was hyperventilating and had to sit. He breathed a few times into a paper bag from Fairway. Then, without hesitation, he agreed to foot the bill if I'd do the dirty work.

We would share possession of *The Day the Clown Cried,* if in fact I found it. Now a "professional," he insisted on writing up a contract. So we scribbled a few terms on the back of his e-mail threat. Then he wrote me a new check and signed it this time.

When I told him the address of my upcoming meeting, he reopened the table drawer. Then Abner placed the gun into my hand.

"Forget it," I said.

"Hey, look, it fooled *you,* didn't it?"

I shrugged, then shoved it into a small side pocket of my pants. Like so many things I possessed, I only wanted it because it was worthless.

Abner walked me to the elevator, which an elegant attendant manned. Despite the disparity in our fortunes, and our mutual hatred, we were partners now. Still, there was one piece of unfinished business.

As the door closed, I said, "I think it's Stanley Lager."

"What do you mean?"

"Who's been trying to kill you."

Before I traveled down, I saw only the faintest recognition in Abner's eyes that this had ever happened. He had bigger fish to fry now.

So did I. Bigger than my mother, I mean. She would have to wait.

THE FLOPHOUSE WHERE THE *CLOWN* MAN STAYED WAS ON WEST THIRTY-sixth Street, not far from my apartment. It was crushed between a bodega and a karaoke club. And The Gladiola smelled anything but sweet.

The lobby looked like a bus station, circa 1952. At least that's what I assumed from seeing movies. There were a few torn leather chairs and a couch the springs of which had long ago burst. The old guy behind the counter probably couldn't remember the last time he washed his hair. When I mentioned Room 54, he only shrugged and pointed me to a nearby stairwell. It stood beside an elevator on which hung a sign that said "BROKEN," complete with misused quotation marks.

As I climbed five flights that smelled of pee, I felt Abner's little gun in my pocket, pressed against my shin. The tense twitching of my eyelid reminded me that I had no idea what I was getting into.

I thought of the uncompleted *Bogart Slept Here,* Mike Nichols's movie of Neil Simon's script, starring Marsha Mason and Robert De Niro. It was scrapped in the seventies for reasons still unclear, though some said De Niro wasn't so funny after doing *Taxi Driver.* It had reemerged, rewritten and recast, as *The Goodbye Girl.*

The fifth-floor stairwell door needed a hard push to open. Then I walked on a chewed-up hall runner, hearing sounds of afternoon TV talk shows and a baby crying. When I reached the door marked 54, it differed conspicuously from the others.

It was open.

Not all the way. It creaked open the second that I placed my knuckles on the wood to knock. Maybe, expecting my appearance, the mystery man had gotten the ball rolling. But no reply came when I raised my voice.

"Hello? Hey, uh," and here I felt stupid, "Ted6569? It's me . . . Roy Milano?"

It was one room, with a bed—still made—a rickety table, and a TV attached to a stand by a chain. A window was covered by a torn and gently blowing blind. The bathroom was to the left.

That was where the breathing came from.

It was labored and inconsistent. Sometimes there was a normal inhale-exhale, then a second of silence, then a wheeze or a moan. It grew louder, then softer, then stopped, then started up again.

It took a few broad steps from the door to get there. It seemed like the longest walk of my life. When I reached the doorway, I peered slowly around it, like a panning camera. But the guy on the bathroom floor wasn't acting.

He was propped up against the can. He was old, in his seventies maybe, wearing an old-guy undershirt, khaki pants, and sneakers that had seen better days. For his age, he was trim and fit. But his face was the color of the gray wall behind him.

He looked up at me, shocked and helpless.

"The other guy . . ." he began to say.

Then his breath came faster and faster before it stopped altogether.

"*WHAT'D* YOU SAY YOU WERE DOING THERE?"

I sat in a precinct interrogation room, before a detective named Florent. I'd been passed off to him by the patrolmen who'd arrived at the scene. (I'd called the police the other time I'd found a dead body, too. Mistake or not, it makes for good citizenship.)

Florent was a stocky, handsome guy of forty with a well-trimmed head of curly gray hair. He seemed only slightly more interested in my answers than the other cops had been. An old man with a flophouse heart attack. A loser who found him. I could tell this case would not be a priority.

"He had a movie I wanted," I mumbled.

Despite my cool demeanor, I felt a sharp pain in my left breast and imagined that it was spreading to my arm. To calm down, I tried a meditation technique I'd seen on a TV infomercial; I was supposed to picture a space between my eyes, or something. When I saw the cop's perplexed expression, I realized I must look like Jerry Lewis in one of his usual roles. So, for comfort, I went back to trivia.

"Clint Eastwood replaced Frank Sinatra in *Dirty Harry,*" I blurted out. "Don Siegel replaced Irvin Kershner as director."

I hadn't meant to say it out loud, but it was too late. The cop nodded, with a thin, impatient smile. Between my crossed eyes and my comment, he must have thought I was a mental patient.

"What kind of movie did he have?" he asked, as if speaking to a foreign child.

Could I risk telling him? Confiding in Abner had been bad enough; the last thing I needed was someone else finding out. But what were the chances of a cop caring about *this* film? Virtually none.

"He said he had *The Day the Clown Cried.*"

"Jerry Lewis's famous, unreleased drama?" he asked.

I closed my eyes and cursed, in silence. The trivial community was growing so large, yet staying so secret, that you never knew who it included. Even cops, apparently, were now part of it. Come to think of it, this guy looked like he could have been an actor once. Well, in high school plays.

"That's the one," I said, almost inaudibly.

"Huh."

"You know your movies."

"I'm a big fan. You know that CD-ROM game? I'm the best."

I smiled, trying to keep my condescension hidden. The trivia game he mentioned was for amateurs, but let the cop have his dream. He was too powerful to be truly trivial.

"Great."

"A lot of people would kill to see that film."

The remark had an edge. Detective Florent wasn't dismissing this case so easily now, I thought, with trepidation. I could offer to cut him in, but the pie was getting awfully thin.

Florent toyed with a baggie that held a scuffed-up, old man's wallet.

"But you say you didn't know the old guy, Ted Savitch?"

I shook my head. "I didn't even know his whole name."

"Well, he knew you."

"Some people do," I shrugged. "I've got a newsletter. Would you like a subscription? It's called *Trivial Man,* and in it, I . . ."

As I'd secretly hoped, the cop's attention waned the more I spoke. No matter how much he liked movies, he occasionally thought of other things. I droned on and on, hoping to bore him to death and, not incidentally, firmly establish how harmless I was. But before he could interrupt to dismiss me, the door opened. A patrolman stuck his head in.

"She's here," he said.

"Great," Florent said, relieved.

He asked me to inform him if I went anywhere. Then, with a last, contemptuous laugh, he added, "But that's not going to happen, is it?"

After he left, I let out a grateful sigh that turned into a racking cough. Above all, I was glad Detective Florent hadn't seen my gun.

I shuffled toward the door of the station house, attacked by a sudden wave of self-disgust. I'd been so desperate that I'd believed Ted Savitch, the dead old man. Why hadn't I just assumed he was a fraud or a nut? I'd been hearing from enough of them lately. He'd probably thought he'd pull a fast one, hand me a phony film, and make a killing. Instead, the stress had killed *him*.

Between my mother, Abner Cooley, and this, my life had become a disaster. I could only look forward to scrounging up some typesetting work.

Yet I couldn't help but wonder: What did Ted Savitch say before he died? "The other guy . . ."? Had he just seen someone else? Who had it been?

I started to open the precinct door. Then I looked to the left, and stopped. Through the glass window of a closed room, I saw a woman, waiting. She was about thirty, slightly built, and kind of peculiar-looking.

"Who's that?" I asked Detective Florent, who was passing by.

He stared at me a second, confused. Then he remembered who I was. "That's his daughter."

"Who?"

"You know," he said. "The dead guy."

Then he went into the room and joined her.

I WAITED ACROSS THE STREET FROM THE PRECINCT. IN A MAGAZINE STORE, I browsed through movie reviews in magazines, checking out the window every few seconds. Just when the proprietor approached to throw me out, I saw the door of the precinct open. Detective Florent was bidding the dead guy's daughter good-bye.

After she left, he shook his head. It was the same kind of dismissive reaction he'd given me. This made me move even faster to follow her.

There was something about the woman's full head of unruly hair—blond with a punk red stripe—and her sensible sweater over torn black tights. She seemed to dress too old and too young for her age, as if she'd gotten advice from all the wrong books. In other words, she looked like the world's rarest and most desired of creatures: a trivial woman.

Or maybe I just hoped she was.

"Excuse me?" I said, panting, when I caught up.

Standing at a light, she looked at me, very slowly. I noticed three things immediately: Her makeup was applied too heavily, another promising sign. She was attractive, in a weird sort of way, with high cheekbones, full lips, and piercing blue-gray eyes. And there were tears all over her face. Well, why wouldn't there be? I thought, suddenly. Her father was just found dead.

"I'm the one who found your dead father," I said.

There was a long pause, as I cursed myself. This wasn't exactly a "meet cute," like in a romantic comedy. I remembered that Cary Grant had turned down Billy Wilder's *Sabrina* and *Love in the Afternoon*. Bogart and Cooper were, respectively, miscast in them, instead.

"Excuse me?" she said.

"I'm sorry," I babbled. "Your father, I . . . I'm the one, the one who . . . his heart attack . . . I . . ."

"Oh. Oh."

To my surprise, she didn't burst into racking sobs. In fact, it seemed *that* part of her day was over. She briskly wiped away what moisture was left on her face.

"I'm sorry," she said, sensibly. "That must have been awful."

"Well, not . . . as bad as for you . . . I mean . . ."

She shrugged. "We weren't close. I hadn't seen him for years."

"Oh. Well, I know what it's like not to . . . get along . . . with your family."

"Do you? That's nice. I mean, it's . . . not nice, but I don't know the right word for what it is. I'm Dena Savitch."

"Roy Milano."

We shook hands. Despite her matter-of-fact demeanor, I could still feel the tears that dampened her palm.

"May I buy you coffee?" she asked.

"Sure. Except let me."

"No," she said, definitively. "I insist."

Dena Savitch also insisted on ordering for both of us. When our coffees came, she popped open the little milk container, sniffed it, then okayed it for my use. I assumed that her reaction to anxiety was to impose order. This was in contrast, of course, to my own obsessive recounting of film facts and stats. There were all kinds of ways to be trivial, I thought, hopefully.

"How did you know my father?" she asked me, bluntly.

"I didn't. He contacted *me*."

"You sell something? Have a business, what?"

Her grilling was unnerving yet kind of charming. "I think he wanted to sell *me* something."

"A service of some kind? Some belongings? I have no idea what my father was into."

After a pause, I decided to plunge in, to definitively see if she shared my way of life. "He said he had *The Day the Clown Cried*."

She paused, but only to unwrap a sugar cube. "What's that? One of those corny clown paintings?"

My heart sank. Had I thought wrong, was she really normal? As I watched Dena crush the sugar with her fist into just the right size sprinkles, I was heartened: right type, wrong topic, maybe.

"It's a famous uncompleted film," I said, and proceeded to explain. I told her how Jerry Lewis's previous film had also been about World War Two: *Which Way to the Front?*, a comedy. As I went on and on, she proceeded to look around the room. Only when I finally trailed off did her attention return. Still, it was clear she'd heard *something*.

"Well," she said, "I guess my father really needed cash."

I stared at her. "You're saying he might have actually *had* it?"

She shrugged. "As I said, I don't know what he's been doing lately. He left my mother when I was little. But he was a movie fan, I remember that."

"It's not enough to be a fan, see, he'd have to be . . ." and off I went again, explaining that Jerry Lewis had done a previous dramatic turn in *The Jazz Singer* on TV in the fifties. This time, Dena's gaze floated upward, and she seemed to count the ceiling tiles. Only when my voice stopped—when I wet my whistle with my now-cool coffee—did she meet my eyes once more. This time, too, she'd heard just enough to respond. She checked me out, analytically.

"I can see why he called you," she said, not unkindly. "Why anyone would have, under those circumstances."

I studied her now. I remembered how, when I was a child, my mother would start doing chores—cleaning, cooking, sorting laundry—whenever I regaled her with trivia. "I'm listening, I'm listening," she would say. Yet I knew she would sometimes sneak off by herself, in the afternoons, to the city, to see films.

For all my attempts to hew Dena to me and mine, maybe she wasn't trivial; she was maternal.

But not necessarily in a bad way.

"Look," she said, suddenly. "I think we can help each other."

I leaned in, believing her; she said nothing frivolously. Dena shifted in her seat, too, and I caught a glimpse of a fallen black bra strap. A faint charge of arousal went through me and, under the circumstances—the memory of my mother—it was unnerving. Staring straight into my eyes, she pulled the strap back up, with what seemed intentional slowness. Fathers and mothers; falling bras and crying clowns; everything seemed to be mingling, in ways I didn't understand. Whatever it was made both of us look away.

But I knew one thing for certain: I trusted Dena Savitch. So I went ahead and told her what I thought.

"I think your father may have died . . . for *The Day the Clown Cried*."

She didn't hesitate.

"Do you?" she said.

"Yes."

"So do I."

Neither of us spoke for a second. Then she said, "Roy? Would you like to go to the Hamptons with me?"

PART 2

THE HAMPTONS

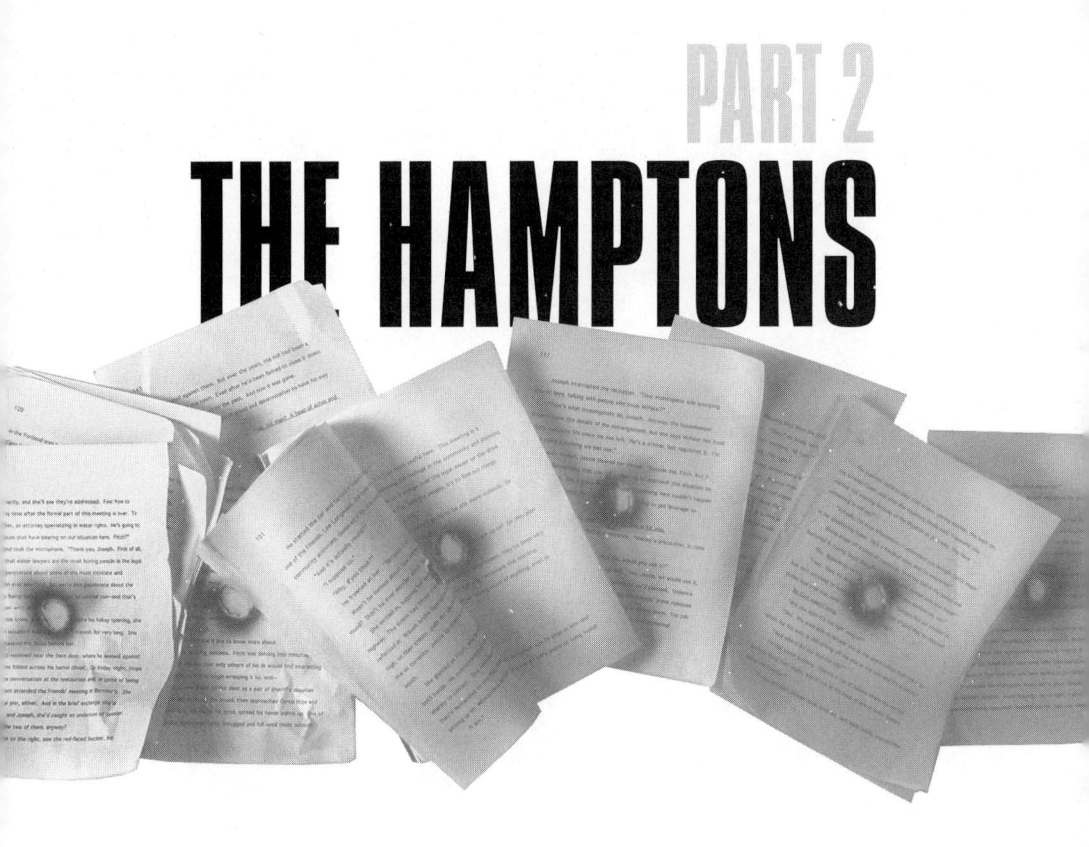

DENA DIDN'T LIVE ON THIS PART OF LONG ISLAND, A WORLD OF MANSIONS on the water, two hours or so from town. She worked for a man of whom, not surprisingly, she had barely heard.

Most people, however, were more than familiar with Howie Romaine.

Romaine was a stand-up comic who had parlayed an observational gift—creating routines from mundane details of everyday life—into an enormous success. He'd recently ended his stupendously popular TV sitcom, *Romaine World,* which had made him untold millions. Now married with a child, he lived in a compound in East Hampton, essentially retired at the age of forty. Dena was the au pair to his young son and lived on the grounds.

The job made sense for her. At lunch, Dena's motherly aspect had made me confess more than I'd intended. I told her of my own mom and my unfortunate alliance with Abner, in such a miserable way that it made her think, as she always seemed to, practically.

"Howie spends all his time buying things now," she'd said. "Fancy cars used to be his obsession. Now he's into showbiz collectibles. So he might have some information on this, whatever, *Clown* film."

I hesitated. Romaine's comic oeuvre had always struck me—and, frankly, anyone with any taste—as pathetic. Who really cared about the rivalry between an electric and a manual toothbrush, as one of his routines dramatized?

Dena read my mind and was, as ever, sensible. "Don't be such a snob. This is a way to keep our investigation going. I'm having my father's belongings from his flophouse shipped to me at Howie's place. You can help me go through them there."

I sensed this was her real motivation and, to my surprise, I didn't mind. It was very comforting being around Dena. She had suffered a greater loss than I—my silent mother was still alive—yet had been made stronger.

"Okay," I found myself saying. "All right."

"Oh," she said, as she paid the check, "and you'll want to lose that gun, I think. I hate those things."

Just as she heard what she needed, Dena saw what she needed, as well.

At home, I stashed the gun in my underwear drawer. Then I logged onto Quelman House. The site featured *An Open Letter from a Special Guest.* Mimicking the gossipy style of Abner's PRINTIT!.com, it read:

> Well, *Quelman* lovers, your cinematic ordeals are over. Prince Corno and Lady Beluga are going to stay a peninsula apart. . . . And what former Internet bigwig is maintaining the integrity of the world's favorite fantasy trilogies? I don't have to *print it* here. . . .

There was a coda:

> And stay tuned. This particular *cool* cat will soon announce his acquisition of one of the world's most lusted-after films. That won't be a day *anyone* cries. . . .

Abner, of course, had written his own tribute. Typically, he had also taken very premature credit for finding the film.

Annoyed, I e-mailed him a vague account of my hotel encounter. Then I told him the address where I was headed, ending with a cursory: *Might get info there.* Then I cashed his check.

I accompanied Dena on the Jitney, the elegant bus line to the Hamptons from Manhattan. On the way, they served complimentary Perrier in plastic cups and gave out copies of the *Wall Street Journal,* a paper I had never read. When I got tired of trying to fold its oversized pages, looking for film reviews, I crumpled it beneath my seat.

I thought that maybe Dena hadn't merely wanted to help me or to receive my help. After what happened to her father, maybe she could use my protection, too. Even though she seemed parental, she was in fact the younger one.

Was I up to it? As I looked out the window at the Long Island Expressway, I thought of Martin Ritt's abandoned film from the early eighties. It starred Sally Field and Matthew Broderick in a May-December romance. It was resurrected as *No Small Affair* starring Demi Moore and Jon Cryer.

There was a limo waiting for us at the East Hampton bus stop. With a hidden driver, it took us through secluded lanes and protective hedges behind which lived the likes of Steven Spielberg and P. Diddy. And Howie Romaine.

In person, Romaine was as tall as he'd seemed on TV. He'd gained a belly and lost some hair since his early retirement, though. His handshake was very weak, as if, now so rich, he no longer needed to make an effort of any kind.

"It's nice to meet a cousin of Dena's," he said, clearly not giving a damn one way or the other. I was just a slacker relation and of no use to him.

Dena thought that, by introducing me as her family, it would eliminate any uncomfortable questions. But Howie, who literally yawned a second after our handshake, was not about to ask any.

I glanced around his massive living room, decorated in conventional leather and plaids. Four Emmy Awards were placed in plain view on a mantel. Dozens of framed photos of his old sitcom cast adorned the walls. There were copies of his recent best seller, *Fatherhood Is No Joke,* the cover of which showed him dandling a baby, lovingly. But only one small shot of his wife and child sat, nearly hidden, on a desk.

"I loved your show," I lied, to win him over.

Howie's eyes brightened, and his whole demeanor changed. He stood up straighter and patted my shoulder and spoke louder. "Thanks, thanks. It was just a little, you know, bagatelle. But it made a lot of people happy. Or at least that's what people say. To me, it was just . . . a romp, you know? But we need romps, that's what people tell me. So thanks, thanks."

"Sure," I said, shrugging, and wincing from his volume.

"Now I'm a family man, though," he went on, unbidden, "and that's how I like it. I don't miss doing the show for a minute. I think people like you miss it a lot more than me!"

He laughed, deafeningly, waiting for confirmation. I only nodded, with a fake smile, not wanting to give him too much. I'd seen his show once, I thought, on a TV in an airport lounge.

"Howie's very interested in talking to you about *The Way the Clown Cried,*" Dena jumped in.

"*The Day,*" I said to my cousin.

"Oh, sure, sure," Howie went on, my big pal now. "I've done some research. I called Jerry Lewis about it, but he hasn't called back. It's a sore spot with him. I'm working on it . . ." he groped for my name.

"Roy."

"I'm working on it, Roy. Did you know that Jerry came to our set one day? All kinds of people did. But these days, I just see my wife, my kid, and the grocery delivery guy. And that's the way I like it."

Howie gave the impression of a man who had already risen to the heights of his life. To his shock, he now found himself, at a relatively young age, still alive and bored to death.

As he spoke, I noticed that he had slipped a hand around Dena's waist and kept it there. She allowed it, clearly uncomfortable. Maybe this was another reason she'd asked me to come: to give Howie something else to think about.

"We'll talk," he said to me. "You'll be here, right? That's right, Dena said so. There's plenty of room in the guest house." My one mild compliment had clearly made him desperate to continue our relationship. He added, with strained excitement that couldn't hide his terrible disappointment, "Right now, though, I have to take my little cutie to the park."

On the last remark, he gave Dena an especially tight squeeze. It took me a second to realize that he had meant his son, whose name he didn't mention.

"I love the slide!" he said shrilly, as he left the room. "That's all I need now! The slide and the swing! That's a full day!"

Howie lasted exactly twenty minutes at the park before he brought his son back for Dena to mind. Then he disappeared into his den to make phone calls to buy more things.

Dena showed exceptional kindness and patience with the boy, who was four. He had been named Elliot, after Howie's neurotic sidekick character on *Romaine World.*

"Where's his mother?" I asked, as Dena helped Elliot color in an enormous, toy-clogged playroom.

"I think today is feet. Or maybe it's fingers, I'm not sure." When I wrinkled my brow in confusion, she explained, "Luna's getting them done."

"Oh."

"Elliot's a nice boy, and he seems to have his father's ability to notice small things. Just yesterday we talked for twenty minutes about how to pull on socks. He's very methodical."

In fact, the boy was coloring very consistently and deliberately. By displaying these qualities, he seemed to take after Dena more than his comical father. Maybe that made sense, given who was really raising him.

She looked up at me then, answering a question I hadn't asked. "I was prelaw. But I never finished my degree."

I perked up at this. Her aimlessness made Dena more a candidate for our community than ever. Maybe all she needed was an area of expertise. Could she discover one by deciphering her father's death?

I was about to find out.

"That's my father's things," she said, hearing the doorbell ring. "This could be the answer we're looking for."

IF HIS BELONGINGS WERE ANY CLUE TO TED SAVITCH'S LIFE, IT WAS ONE lived on the go.

In the boxes and envelopes were bills from utilities in different states. Receipts of purchases from New York to Denver to Palo Alto. Paycheck stubs from jobs that ranged from bookkeeper to cashier to movie theater manager.

Dena's father favored undershirts and pleated pants. He read copiously, whether it was history or classic fiction or movie star biographies. He took pills for his heart. His last-known address seemed to have been in Bar Harbor, Maine.

There were a few blurred and torn photographs. They were all of a little girl, taken from a distance, in public places. Dena's eyes filled with tears when she saw these.

"Look. That's me as a kid," she said. "He must have taken them secretly. Then I guess he ran away again."

As was her wont, Dena willed herself to stop crying and brushed the tears away. Then she carried on with the business at hand. She turned one picture over. On the back, her father had written Dena's name with various phone numbers, crossing out each one as they changed over the years. It was how the police had found her, I figured.

"He kept track of me," she said, quietly.

There were no videotapes, let alone any mention of *The Day the Clown Cried.* But there was, on the bottom of the last box, a copy of my newsletter, *Trivial Man*.

Dena and I didn't speak for a while. She had clearly been shaken by the shabby facts of her father's life, as well as his continuing interest in her. I was disappointed and confused by the lack of any clues. Finally, she broke the silence with typical hardheadedness.

"So, do you think," she said, "that someone was at my father's room before you?"

"Looks like it," I replied. "He said, 'The other guy . . . ' "

"Did he have any marks of . . . I don't know— He wasn't bleeding or anything?"

I shook my head.

"So it was like someone had just threatened him?"

"Right."

"Or not. You said his door was open?"

"Yes."

"So someone could have just walked in? I mean, it could have been a mistake. And he just overreacted?"

"Possibly. You *should* have been a lawyer."

Dena smiled and blushed, slightly. Besides her tears, it was the first sign of normal vulnerability I had noticed. We were seated on a couch in Howie's expansive guest house, easily twice the size of my apartment. She shifted, shyly, on the pillow beside me. Again, her bra strap slowly fell. This time, she didn't retrieve it. She stared squarely into my eyes and heat covered my face. Then, again, both of us looked away.

"I was going to be a *patent* lawyer, silly," she said, as if saying the merriest, flirtiest thing imaginable. Then she left the room.

That night I took the couch while Dena slept a few feet away, behind a screen. At first, I fell into a fitful sleep. Then the strange bed, plus the pressure of my new assignment, caused me to bolt awake. As usual, I recounted trivia, as opposed to counting sheep. I had become immersed in the world of abandoned films, so I segued to the subject of replaced actors.

"Peter O'Toole replaced Albert Finney in *Lawrence of Arabia . . .*" I mumbled. "Jack Nicholson replaced Mandy Patinkin in *Heartburn . . .*"

From behind Dena's screen, I heard people speaking now. A man and woman whispered, he more vociferously than her. As I strained to hear, I made out the not-so-funny tones of Howie Romaine.

Though I couldn't understand his words, he had the unmistakable sound of a man begging, pleading, and cajoling for sex. After he subsided, the woman—it had to be Dena—responded with what seemed familiar, calm resistance.

". . . not the best idea . . ." were the only words of Dena's I could discern. Then, undaunted, Howie continued whispering his wants and needs.

He must have crept in during the brief time I slept. I was sure it wasn't the first time, either. From the sound of Dena's voice, I sensed he had never been successful in his quest.

Why should he be now? Wasn't that part of the reason I was there? After all, what was family for?

"Bette Davis replaced Mary Pickford in *Storm Center . . .*" I grumbled, much louder now. "Robert Preston replaced Marlon Brando in Sidney Lumet's *Child's Play . . .*"

There was silence behind the screen. Then, "What the hell is that?" Howie hissed.

"My cousin," Dena answered.

"Well, what's he— Who's he talking to?"

"No one. He's talking in his sleep."

"Jesus Christ."

"Jeff Daniels replaced Michael Keaton in *The Purple Rose of Cairo . . .*" I went on, even louder. "Elizabeth Taylor replaced Vivien Leigh in *Elephant Walk . . .*"

"This is impossible," Howie said, his own volume rising. "I can't even hear myself think!"

I can't even hear myself beg would have been funnier, I thought. But who gave notes to Howie Romaine?

I threatened to start a new list. Before I could, I saw the tall, potbellied shadow of the comic, dressed only in a T-shirt and shorts, dart from behind the screen and out the door.

There was silence for a while. Then, very quietly, Dena said, "Thanks."

"No problem," I replied.

I realized that Dena might be looking for something besides protection or an explanation of her father's death. Maybe she wanted a piece of the *Clown*, too. It would be a windfall for most people—not for me, of course; I just wanted to see it and tell others—but for normal people. Dena could use the money to get out of her present situation, babysitting a lonely boy and resisting a restless man. We all had our secret needs; that's why there were contracts and negotiations—and guns. Was I in a position where one day she would owe me something?

"Good night, Roy," she said, but I didn't reply.

Money wasn't foremost on Howie's mind, either; he had enough of it. I could tell the next day, when he took me into his garage.

His garages. They were the size of yet another house beside his Tudor-style mansion. Climate controlled, evocatively lit, they served to brilliantly house and highlight his collection of cars.

Apparently there were priceless Porsches and BMWs, plus a few vintage Jaguars. I couldn't drive, didn't care about cars—they didn't even qualify as trivia—and so I just nodded, politely, as he described them.

Howie seemed to perceive my indifference, because "That one's an Aston Martin," he said to engage me. "Like in James Bond."

My grunt of recognition was only slightly louder.

It had been awhile since I complimented him. Howie had tried ingratiating himself to me, his unreceptive audience. Now, ever the performer, he became more aggressive and turned the tables.

"So what was your favorite? Episode, I mean? Of *Romaine World*?"

I froze now, as Howie blithely spat into a rag and started rubbing a car. I racked my brain for any of Howie's routines, which always served as bases for his shows, but could only remember the one.

"The one," I said, "about the toothbrush."

There was a long and terrifying pause. Howie stopped rubbing, turned, and stared at me. Then he slowly started to smile.

"Wow," he said, appreciatively. "That's incredible."

"Oh, yeah," I agreed, sweating, "it was."

"No, because, well, of course, you know why."

My heart starting to beat faster, I considered even bringing the conversation back to cars. But Howie came to my rescue.

"Because 'Toothbrush' was only shown once. It's not included in the syndication package. Because, you know, of the line about the Europeans."

"Ohh," I said, nodding. "Of course."

"Leave it to you to choose the lost episode!"

I had passed with flying colors. Howie put an arm around my shoulder and pulled me close. He rubbed my hair affectionately, as if I were his son. I assumed he'd never done this to his own little boy.

"How'd you like it," he said, and even called me, "kid?"

"How'd I like what?" I was all bunched up in his arms now.

" 'Toothbrush.' The episode. I'll get you a dub."

"Great," I said, and tried to sound thrilled. While there were people who would have swooned at the idea, sitcom trivia was way down on my list.

The idea fired Howie up, however. "Truth be told, Roy, I've come to the end with my car thing. I'm writing a whole new chapter. I'm going to start with the famous lost episode of *Romaine World,* then I'll buy *The Day the Clown Cried,* then everything else. All the lost entertainments. Price will be no object." The garage seemed to shrink and decay right before his eyes. "I'm going to pull out the garages and build a theater, that's what I'm going to do!"

His breath was coming fast; I was almost concerned for his health, given his recent dissipation. Then he calmed down, as if he sensed it was unseemly. "My little cutie will love it," he added, carefully. "We'll watch all the Disney stuff."

The Day the Clown Cried would keep Howie with his family, down on the farm, as it were. I felt vaguely nauseated by his motive for wanting it. And impatient to learn what he knew.

But there was no time to ask him. Howie was opening a door to one of his cars.

"Take the Jag," he said, "out for a spin."

I just stared. I didn't know if this was another test or a mad gesture of generosity. Either way, my left shoulder started to twitch, and I thought that Richard Crenna had replaced Kirk Douglas in *First Blood* opposite Sylvester Stallone.

"I don't drive," I said.

"Of course you do." Howie couldn't conceive of such a thing. "It's a seventy-two, same year as Jerry's film. Here's the registration." He was pulling out cards. "And if the cops stop you"—he scribbled on the back of one—"just show them this."

Howie's note read: "Don't say I didn't warn you!" After a second for alarm, I realized it was a catchphrase from his show.

There was no way to resist. Howie pushed me—not so gently—inside the giant brown Jag. I landed on its burnished leather front seat. Slowly, I buckled an old-fashioned, across-the-gut belt. The key was already in the ignition. When I turned it, the car hummed, deafeningly.

"Doesn't it sound great?" Howie asked.

"It's a beaut!" I cried.

I had driven occasionally—reparked my aunt Ruby's car just the other week—but never for an extended "spin." As I backed out, the screech of my brake and gas stamping couldn't have made Howie happy.

He didn't seem to care, though. He was too busy fumbling in his pocket and bringing out a cigarette.

"Don't tell Luna," he said, pointing to the smoke. The warning was no joke; he valued his remaining pleasures; I could tell from the look in his eye.

I started out of his driveway, which was the length of a private lane.

Howie and his house were soon specks in my rearview, which I didn't know how to adjust.

I came out onto a silent road, where other massive homes hid behind their hedges. I intended to drive one block, park, wait twenty minutes, then return.

Right away, though, I abandoned my plan.

I was being followed.

IT WAS THE ONLY OTHER CAR ON THE ROAD. IT SEEMED TO HAVE COME OUT of nowhere. Had it been waiting for me?

I could barely make it out in my obstructed rearview. It wasn't a collectible, that was for sure. It was a grubby white Honda with a dent in its side.

It kept a discreet distance. To lose it, I took a right turn. I saw no one else as I drove, never even glimpsed a house behind the walls of foliage. I could be killed, I realized, in this most exclusive of neighborhoods, and have no witness.

My companion dogged me, always far enough away to avoid being seen. I thought I made out a man at the wheel, but even that, in the half-sight the mirror afforded me, was unclear.

I began to smell water. I suspected that, blindly driving in this expensive maze, I was heading toward the ocean. I knew that beach property was the most desirable and the most secluded: a dead end.

Trying to avoid being cornered, I took a sudden left. I was alone on a road for a minute. I dared to go faster, watching my speed hit twenty, then thirty. Had I lost him? Then I heard a shocking sound: the squeal of wheels as the other car hung the same sharp louie and came after me.

It wasn't kidding anymore. My early awkward speed may have been charming; my new attempt at escape was not. The car went faster and faster, came closer and closer; I could hear the sputter of its cheap or aging engine. I remembered that James Cagney had replaced a guy named Edward Woods in *Public Enemy*; the two switched roles, making Cagney a star.

I remembered something else: This wasn't my car. The thought occurred to me because the Honda was just about to ram my ass.

Then it slammed on its brakes, suddenly. A car was coming from the other direction.

A brand-new, gleaming Mercedes was—I can only call it—"tootling" toward us. A middle-aged lady in a mink was gabbing on a cell phone, obliviously. She didn't see my frantic waving. Never even looking my way, she turned the corner and disappeared.

But someone else saw my motioning for help: the man in the Honda. Once the road was clear, he took his chance again. Spinning his wheels, gunning his motor, he flew full force into the back of Howie Romaine's expensive ride.

Wearing only the thirty-year-old seat belt, I flew into the steering wheel, my head a bare inch from the windshield. My chest burning, the sound of smashed bumper in my ears, I ricocheted back into my bucket seat, my shoulders seared.

On the deserted road, the other car began to back up for another go.

Like an enraged bull, it seemed to stomp its feet and pant before it sped forward once more. The second of preparation gave me time to spin the wheel left, cutting into the oncoming lane, to get away.

I was heading right into what I now recognized as a Porsche.

The guy behind this wheel was also talking on a cell phone. He was middle-aged, suntanned, and wearing a Polo shirt, collar up. My full-speed approach shocked him off his call, and, shrieking like a chicken, he chucked the gadget into his backseat.

Frantically stroking my wheel all the way left, I crossed his path, barely missing him. Then I brushed a hedge, shearing off green shards, before completing a half-circle back to the right lane.

Sweating and wincing—too stunned to even breathe, which hurt like hell—I floored the pedal of the giant old car. I heard a rattle from my rear end and realized that my tormentor had done more damage than I had known.

He wasn't finished with me, either. He was coming again at full gallop.

We were moving swiftly into a more populated area. Houses were becoming visible, closer together, and smaller. I yearned for ocean smell and solitude. I had been a fool not to take my chances there. Ahead of me was a stop sign. Beyond that was a busy four-way intersection.

I had a choice: I could slam on my brakes, feel his full impact, and go right into the windshield. Or I could barrel through the stop sign, get hit by cars from all four sides, be crushed and killed.

The choice was taken from me. My foot was frozen on the gas.

I zoomed through the sign. I pulsed luckily past a car coming from my right. One coming left, though, snagged my back door and spun itself around. I tried to steer away from the one coming at me, but my left headlight cracked deafeningly into its right.

The impact jarred me. I lost control, was propelled onto a sidewalk, then halfway up a shiny, green, trimmed lawn. The German shepherd sleeping there reared up and, barking in dismay, raced into a backyard.

The pedal brake was useless. I grappled desperately for the emergency. Not finding it, I yanked the gearshift into park, stripping it, noisily.

I stopped.

I tried to catch my breath. Then I looked behind me.

Zipping by in the street was the Honda. As it drove away, I saw the man at the wheel.

He was a clown. Or someone with a white clown's face.

NO MATTER HOW MANY CARDS I GAVE THE COP, HE DIDN'T BELIEVE I KNEW Howie Romaine.

"But—" I said, as he was hauling me out on my feet, " 'Don't say you weren't warned!' That's what Howie always—"

" 'Don't say I didn't *warn you,'* " the cop corrected me, disgustedly.

"Whatever. But that's what Howie always—"

He quickly had me turned around, spread-eagled, and pressed against the totaled Jag. Other cars in the accident stood, smoking and impaired, in the street near the lawn. The drivers were too scared of me to come any closer. The home's owner even hid, growling German shepherd at her side, behind her screen door.

"If you're such a good pal of Howie's," the cop said, "what's his phone number?"

Of course, I didn't remember. But I knew what neighborhood I was in and assumed I knew its rules.

"I'm afraid I can't give out his private number," I said, my lips pressed on the side door glass.

"That's a hot one," the cop replied.

My face was now pushed as if to burst through onto the backseat. My hands were jerked behind me, cracked upward, and joined by metal cuffs. I marveled at how far one's arms could be stretched skyward before they broke. It made me think of *Something's Got to Give,* the famous last, lost film of Marilyn Monroe. Also starring Dean Martin, it was abandoned when she was fired—and right before she killed herself. It later became *Move Over, Darling* with Doris Day and James Garner. Everything could be remade in show business, even madness, suicide, and death.

Clearly everyone today wished I was recast as someone unthreatening. How could I assure them that I was harmless?

Someone did it for me.

"He's fine, leave him be."

It wasn't Howie. It was Dena, who now stood—I figured, for I couldn't turn around—beside the cop.

"Who says?" he answered.

I heard feet crunch grass and gravel as Dena and the cop moved away. Their discussion became muted, private, worldly. I heard the cop say "Oh, sure, okay," as if he were reminded of the rules that voided tickets, cleared records, and let people go.

In a minute, my hands were free.

Dena drove me in one of Howie's other cars—the coupe, I think. I saw the rich people in the street staring after me, as if I were a frightening alien who had landed on their world.

"I *told* Howie I couldn't drive," I said, quietly.

"He's not the best listener," Dena nodded. "As you could tell last night."

She blushed a little, then shook it off. She was in her usual conflicted outfit: an old-lady blouse over teenage, low-slung jeans. When we reached a stop sign—the same one I had failed to obey—she reached over and touched my hot, red face.

"When I heard, I came looking for you," she said. "Are you all right?"

"Sort of." Then I told her. "But I think someone just tried to kill me for *Clown*."

When I checked my e-mail on Dena's laptop, I saw several impatient messages from Abner. They all essentially asked the same questions: Had I found the film? Why hadn't I answered him? I typed in a generic reply: "Still working on it." Then I added: "Howie even less funny than on TV." Then I logged off.

In truth, I was less concerned about Abner than about Howie. How much could I tell the comic about the danger involved in finding *Clown*? Should I get him to tell me what he knew first? How long would that take, anyway? And, not incidentally, what would he say when he saw his car?

"Like I told you," he shrugged the next morning, as he watched a tow truck bring back its remains, "I've come to the end with my car thing."

We were both standing at the open entrance to a garage. He walked farther inside, without even asking about my injuries. Wearing a T-shirt and shorts, he rolled a tennis racket in his hand.

"Where are your whites?" he said.

"Excuse me?"

"Your whites. You play, right?" he called now. He had started toward another car, one I actually recognized as a BMW.

Howie was sure a kidder. "About as well as I drive."

"What?" He was almost out of range.

"I said, you bet your life!" I called.

"Groucho!" he said, disappearing inside the vehicle. "I'll find *his* episodes!" Then he poked his head out. "So wear some of mine!"

To my horror, I found I had been enlisted to play a tennis match for charity with Howie. It wasn't at the court in his backyard, which always stood empty now, as he arranged more purchases. It was at a country club nearby—in other words, in public. Dena couldn't protect me; it was Luna's day for "knuckles and knees," and she was busy minding their son.

"I don't think your shorts really fit," I said, readjusting them, as I sat beside Howie, in the Beamer.

"Hey, *I'm* the baggy pants comic!" he said, chuckling. He thought a minute, then started on a zany comparison between boxers and briefs that made me zone out.

"I just came up with that," he said about the routine, lighting another secret smoke. "I better knock it off, right?"

Like an addict, Howie was threatening to backslide into his bad habit—his career. Did he want me to stop his creativity, or encourage him to continue? I wasn't sure, so I didn't answer. As usual, my lack of response made him hostile. He patted my knee, sore from the crackup, too roughly.

"Hope you got a backhand!" he said, vindictively. "You're gonna need it against Fitzgerald!"

I shrugged, still not speaking. I couldn't think of a living celebrity with that name; Barry Fitzgerald was dead.

Howie pushed my sore shoulder. "Mike Fitzgerald, dummy!"

Sweat slowly started flowing beneath my arms.

"*Mike* Fitzgerald?"

"Yep, The Terrible Rebel. He and Ludwig are playing us. Some group, right?"

Mike Fitzgerald had been number one in the sport in the 1970s and early eighties. His temper and on-court shenanigans had earned him the nickname The Terrible Rebel. Ludwig, I assumed, was Thor Ludwig, the former German champion currently being hounded for unpaid taxes. He was the ex-husband of former child star Gratey McBride. That was the extent of my tennis knowledge. Besides that I would rather die than play them, of course.

"I met them at Troy Kevlin's house in L.A.," he said, mentioning a once-hot and now-defamed Hollywood producer. "We hit a few on Troy's court. Before the drug thing and Troy lost his house."

Howie got what he wanted out of me: a rise. "Look—"

But he cut me off, calming down. "Relax, it's for charity, it's just for fun. Maybe I'll get Thor and the Rebel to go in with me on trivia!"

My friend again, Howie pinched my cheek, as he pulled into the palatial Four Waters club. When he got out, he goofily kissed the forehead of the valet.

"Don't tell Luna!" he told me, this time kidding.

The place was filling up with fancy Hamptons people, all casually decked out. I tried to keep up with Howie, going up a path. He plowed ahead, waving to photographers.

Among the crowd I saw people with faces painted green, in a parody of football yahoos. Suddenly, I thought one of their faces was white, clown-white, like the guy in the Honda.

I was whisked along before I could be sure.

"Too bad we can't hit a few before Mike and Thor get here," Howie said.

"What do you mean? Where?"

We emerged at a giant court, around which huge makeshift bleachers had been erected, already filled with press and people.

"Center court!" Howie said.

As soon as we came out, a sudden roar of approval exploded from the fans. Howie seemed stunned. He went stock-still and his head shot up, like a dying plant receiving water. He had been starving for this kind of attention, I knew. I only hoped he wasn't being overwatered and wouldn't die as a result. His face was already beet red without a point being played.

"Jesus," he murmured. "Willya look at this?"

Soon I sensed it wasn't Howie's safety that was in jeopardy; it was mine. The people with the painted faces were up in the cheap seats. I swore again I saw a white face amid the green. Then the sun shifted and ended my view.

"Play ball!" someone shouted.

MY SHORTS NEARLY FALLING DOWN, I STOOD ACROSS A NET FROM MIKE Fitzgerald and Thor Ludwig. In early middle age, the first was curly-haired and wiry, the second blond and lanky. Both looked like they'd been awake since the late seventies.

I was apparently Howie's doubles partner. Or someone resembling me was. I heard an announcer shouting at the crowd.

"The Terrible Rebel and the Mighty Thor . . . face Howie Romaine and Ray Romano!"

There was a pause of confusion, as the audience realized that I wasn't the popular comic. The correction soon came.

"Movie critic Ray Milizano!"

The two tennis champs approached the net, to shake our hands. The sun went behind a cloud, and I squinted past them, at the stands. Now all the painted faces seemed green. Was I losing my mind?

As my hand was pulled and pumped by one, then two—surprisingly powerful—grips, I felt my heart lurch. The white face was now visible, sitting in a more secluded seat.

Neither of our opponents paid any more attention to me.

"They still love ya, Howie," Mike Fitzgerald said, a multimillionaire still affecting a lower-class New York accent.

"*Our* ovation was only, how do you call it, so-so," Thor added, a multilinguist still affecting a foreigner's unease.

"Ah." Howie shrugged it off. "They just feel sorry for me."

"No, I'm telling ya," Mike said. "You ought to reconsider this retirement thing."

"Take it from me," Thor agreed. "It's important to keep having, what's the word, discretionary income."

Howie pooh-poohed this, putting a brutal grip on my shoulder. "I'm gonna be in trivia collectibles from now on. Just like Roy here."

Both of the former sports stars looked at me, incredulous. Who was *I* to be dictating the future of the great Howie Romaine? Howie was starting ever-so-slowly to blame *me* for his situation, I thought, and now he had his friends' help.

"Well," Mike said, disgustedly, "he must have *something* going for him, that's all I can say."

The announcer, impatient with all the schmoozing at the net, blared again.

"The Terrible Rebel . . ." he repeated, comically, "and the Mighty Thor will play . . ."

The crowd chuckled as Mike gave one of his trademark scowls at the booth. This had struck fear in his opponents twenty-five years ago; now it was just shtick that brought a big laugh from the crowd. Then Mike yelled his old catchphrase, now a parody of his youthful rage: "You're kiddin' me!"

The crowd went wild. One fan wasn't laughing, though. Far above us, I thought I saw the clown-face man make his fingers into a gun. Then he pulled it back and took a stylized shot at me.

What did I fear most: being humiliated or killed? In this arena, I now feared both. I remembered that Stanley Kubrick had replaced Anthony Mann as director of *Spartacus.*

Howie unkindly gave me the coin to toss for serving rights. I spun it nervously across the net, hitting Mike in the ear. The crowd gave a comical *whooo,* but Mike's face showed me his anger was no parody.

"Sorry," I said, but couldn't be heard above the din.

Because Mike had been injured, he and Thor got to choose. They served first. I was sent to the net by Howie, who patted my butt—painfully—with his racket, much to the crowd's delight. I stood there, my attention diverted to the stands. The man from the Honda was fumbling in a bag. Or was it a woman with her purse?

"Bend your knees!" Howie called to me, convulsing everyone.

I did as he told me, with an old, buried sense memory of day camp. Across the net, the German, innovator of the modern booming serve in tennis (I later learned), was winding up. He was out of practice, clearly stiff, and he stopped midtoss several times.

"You're kiddin' me!" Mike yelled at *him* now, getting more laughs.

The man in the stands was pulling something out of his bag. Then a latecomer crossed his path, blocking my—and his—view.

Then a bullet landed at my feet.

It wasn't a bullet, it was a ball. What was probably Thor's weakest serve ever hit like machine-gun fire near my sneaker, sending me backward with a shout of horror. The ball pinged off the court and flew at full-force into the stands.

"Fifteen-love!" the announcer yelled.

Mike and Thor high-fived each other. I turned with an apologetic shrug to Howie, but he was busy betraying me to the crowd.

"'Don't say I didn't warn you!'" he crowed his own catchphrase at them. The resulting hysteria made Howie grin broadly, his face growing even redder.

"Not since Elliot has Howie had such a foil!" the announcer cried, comparing me to Howie's sitcom pal.

Thor was bouncing his ball low to the ground, in anticipation of another blast. The man in the stands now sat directly above his shoulder, a dangerous dot. Something was gleaming in his hand, I was sure. He was starting to raise it, to aim it.

Then, excitedly, someone stood up in front of him.

I didn't see Thor serve. I was hit in the face, in the left cheek. I went down like a dancer in a cruel ballet.

"Thirty-love!"

I lay on the hard court in a fetal position, completely dazed. Soon I felt a foot kick lightly into my behind, and I heard the crowd crack up.

"*He's* who you're gonna be like?" Mike called to Howie, just between celebs.

"Go figure," Howie answered. Then I heard him counting, loudly, like a fight referee. "One! . . . Two! . . . Three!"

On four, to belly laughs, I stumbled to my feet. It felt like a match was being played inside my head now. I couldn't remember who Danny Kaye replaced in *White Christmas*. Was it Fred Astaire?

"Come on, Fred Astaire," Howie said. "There's only two sets and five games to go."

When I was erect again, I saw the blurry form of a pale-faced man in the stands, pointing a camera at me. Maybe *this* was who I'd been fearing all along!

Another ball crashed into my crotch then. Pain and nausea filled my frame, as I turned to the side, falling to my knees.

"Forty-love!"

I only had the strength to lift my head and try to check the stands. The photographer was pointing his camera down, below the bleachers, and was feverishly snapping something.

It was a man in white face, making his escape—and, I guessed, a good photo, too.

The crowd was laughing again. I saw that, on the other court, Mike and Thor were doing funny seventies disco dancing, in tribute to their time of fame. In a second, Howie, my own partner, had jumped the net to join them.

I didn't even bother rising from my knees for the next serve, which kissed the line, far from my feet, groin, and face. Howie had served it himself.

"Game to Terrible and Thor!" the announcer yelled. "And Howie!"

My patron had ganged up against me, but I didn't care. I was busy checking out the photographer, to memorize his position. He was sitting beside a lean and beautiful black woman, her face covered by big sunglasses.

I was going to need his film.

"HEY, WAIT FOR ME!"

Howie wouldn't even drive me back.

Pumped up by the match, he sped off alone in his car, waving to adoring fans. I was left standing by myself, as the parking lot emptied out. Finally, I flagged a limo, which was among the last to leave.

In my sweaty whites, I was crushed on a huge backseat, in a gaggle of beautiful hangers-on, roadies, and toadies. Across from me, his head on a model's shoulder, was Thor Ludwig. Showered and dressed, exhausted by what was apparently his first exertion in years, he was dead asleep, snoring quietly.

I sat between two sports fans, a stunning black woman of thirty-five with a thick German accent, and a platinum blond gay man, also foreign. They talked over me in many tongues.

It was only when I noticed the fancy leather bag on the man's lap that I knew: It was the woman from the stands and her photographer friend.

"Excuse me," I got up the courage to say.

The woman, in mid-monologue, stopped talking. She looked over at me, quizzically. Then, with a long leather boot, she lightly kicked at the shin of sleeping Thor, across from her.

"Who's *he*?" I think she asked, in German.

Thor's eyes fluttered open, very slightly. It took him a second to place me. Then, speaking English, he said, "A friend of Howie's." He added a word in German that I think, from the snort that accompanied it, meant *putz*.

The woman shrugged, as if to say, so what? A vote of confidence, I thought. Meanwhile, Thor kept speaking, as if I weren't there.

"Howie's trying to find some film. *The Day the Clown Died*."

"*Cried*," I said, quietly, but no one cared. I was exasperated that Howie had been telling everyone about it.

Thor went back to sleep, snuggling on a fur shoulder. The German woman looked over at me, with surprising interest. "What's this, this movie?"

I waited to respond, calculating how much to reveal. Then I figured, what the hell. I began telling her the story of the film and, as usual, went far beyond the central facts.

"In later years, Ingmar Bergman didn't use Harriet Andersson so much. His leading lady, of course, was usually Liv Ullmann. In his 1978 picture with her, *The Serpent's Egg*, David Carradine replaced Richard Harris. A year or so before, Harris had been replaced by Oliver Reed in *Burnt Offerings* . . ."

I only kept going because the woman didn't interrupt. She also didn't yawn, laugh, or direct her attention elsewhere.

"I prefer Richard Harris," she actually said.

I was speechless, hearing this. I stammered out, "Yes, I guess, on balance, I do, too."

There was a pause. She smiled at me, her long eyelashes going hypnotically up and then down. Encouraged, I went on.

"Liv Ullmann was so big in the early Seventies that she was cast in *Forty Carats*. It was supposed to be Elizabeth Taylor, which would have made more sense."

Amazingly, she was still attentive. I could feel her leather pant leg pressed against my bare thigh. Then, in her accent, she spoke with the pleasant suggestiveness of a Marlene Dietrich.

"I don't meet so much," she said, "the nerd."

I nodded, very slowly, looking at her long, smooth, copper-colored neck. Obviously, I was tempted to keep the conversation going. Still, she was probably just a bored socialite trying to kill a limo ride. And the unexpected intimacy afforded me another opportunity.

"Your friend," I said, hesitatingly, nodding over to my other side, "he took pictures of the match?"

She shrugged, cutely. Then, reaching across me, giving me a full whiff of her perfume, she tapped her friend on the arm. Then she asked him the same question in—was it Dutch?

Her pal pointed to his leather bag and nodded. Then he pressed his own leg, much less pleasantly, against my other bare thigh.

"What," he said, sort of in English, "you want prints?"

"Well, no, not really. See, I—"

"Too bad. Digital," he said. Then he made a sweeping hand gesture and gave a *whooshing* sign. "All wiped out."

I sighed, very deeply. I was about to ask him if he'd seen a clown—or a mime, pronounced *meem*—when the limo came to a sudden halt. One of its massive doors opened, and I saw the gate to Howie's driveway.

"We're going on to the city," my new female friend said, sweetly. "But it was very nice to meet you."

There seemed nothing underhanded or even complicated about her friendliness. I found myself extending my hand to her, very sincerely.

"Roy Milano," I said.

"Marthe Ludwig," she replied.

The name stopped me, my hand still holding hers. Then I felt a finger tap my shoulder.

"Thanks," Thor said, from behind me, "for taking care of my wife."

I turned around, uneasily, afraid to find his fist in my face. But Thor was leaning forward, with great, creaking effort, to shake my hand, too. He turned it into an athlete's grip, our thumbs intertwined.

"Nice match, man," he said, clearly not recalling it.

Within a second, I was on the street. I thought that Thor had certainly changed partners since divorcing Gratey McBride. The limo pulled away, one of its windows slightly down. Thor's wife made the charades gesture that meant moviemaking. Then she waved at me with—could it be true?—actual fondness.

The next night, Dena's backrub was not so fond. It had less to do with my description of Marthe Ludwig—about whom I guessed I gushed—than with my aching back, legs, and arms.

"If it doesn't hurt," she said, squeezing and pounding me, "it's not helping."

That seemed to describe Dena's approach to life in general. She didn't spare herself, either, as karate-chopping my lower back, she assessed her quest for her father's story.

"I guess I'm a lot like him. Going from one thing to another."

"You at least tried," I said, wincing, "to become a lawyer."

She ignored this pep talk. "If this person chasing you is the same one who confronted him . . . there's a lot I still don't know."

I nodded. "It's true. Like, for instance . . . if it *is* the same guy, and he stole *Clown* from your father, what does he want from me now? And if your father *didn't* have *Clown,* and so this guy *didn't* steal it, what does he want from me now?"

Dena relaxed her fingers then, keeping a gentle hold of my shoulders. Her hold on her life was just as tentative, I figured. Maybe she wanted to resolve her father's past purely for herself; otherwise, she couldn't get on with anything. Was I just the vehicle to help her? With Dena resting on my back, I was reminded of a child riding on a flying dragon, something out of *The Seven Ordeals of Quelman*. Maybe it was the painkillers talking.

I turned over, slowly, not wishing to fling her away. We ended up with Dena on my stomach, her punk hair undone, falling in my face. There was no more question of straps or shoulders; she was braless through her middle-aged silk shirt.

She moved her hair out of her eyes. She began to descend toward me and not for more Shiatsu. I began to lean up, to meet her. Then we both stopped. As before, something curtailed our interaction.

And it wasn't just Howie.

"Hey, Roy!" he was calling through the closed door. "Come on! Let's go!"

Howie claimed he had already told me; of course, he hadn't. After being forced to drive his car and return his serve, I would never have agreed to go with him to a comedy club.

"It's where I got my start," he said, as we barreled along the Long Island Expressway in his least ostentatious car, an SUV. "Smirk's is the club where I first told a joke."

"But why are we going there *now*?" It was already nine at night, and the club was in Manhattan.

Howie took this as a jibe, which it was, but it was also a fair question. "I like to see what the new people are doing. There something wrong with that? My kid's asleep, Luna's on the phone. What am I supposed to do, play Scrabble with *you*?"

Howie's hostility was rearing its ugly head more and more often. I worried that we hadn't even formally discussed our main topic, and our relationship had already disintegrated. With me hardly saying a word.

"Look," I said, shouting over the rushing air, "maybe we ought to talk about the . . . you know, *Clown*. What you know about *Clown*."

"We'll do that," he said, defensively. "It's not going to kill you to have a little fun first."

It was a long way to go for fun—it took over two hours to reach the city. Howie parked in an expensive garage near Penn Station, a few blocks from where The Gladiola Hotel, Ted Savitch's last address, stood in ruins. Smirk's Comedy Club was on Fortieth, with a big yellow flag out front, featuring cartoon lips, pursed in amusement.

"I just want to see a couple of sets," he said, as we went in. "You might actually enjoy it."

If his reception at the tennis match was tumultuous, here Howie was greeted with silence. It wasn't indifferent; it came from shock, disbelief, and reverence. In the dark, smoky club, open mouths and staring eyes followed Howie Romaine.

We sat at a table in the back, around which several young comics soon swarmed. Their faces were all obscured in the dim light. Howie shushed them, pointing to a comic now onstage and losing the crowd's attention.

"Let's show a little respect," he whispered.

When the sweating headliner was through, Howie led the applause, putting fingers in his mouth to whistle. Then he allowed himself to hold court.

Free drinks were sent to him; so were plates of fried calamari and stuffed mushrooms. Howie lifted a drink to a nearby bartender, in thanks.

"So, old-timer," one lean young comic panted, in a humorous Old West accent, "what brings you back to these parts?"

The boyish questioner had taken a risk by being familiar and funny. After a scary pause, Howie smiled at him—a little.

"Just seeing what you guys are up to," he said. He didn't compete for laughs with the kid; he didn't have to. The answer made all the others at the table nod, as if hearing something wise.

"You here to try out some new stuff?" another asked, sycophantically.

Howie shook his head, definitively. "No way. Those days are over. I'm a family man now. And a trivia collector. Just like him. If you can believe it."

He waved a limp, contemptuous hand at me. The others nodded, with mild curiosity, then stared again at Howie.

Howie went on. "You know, like *The Day the Clown Cried*."

Privately, I rolled my eyes at his lack of discretion. And in a comedy club, too, where the movie would hardly be unknown!

"Jerry's unreleased film?" one asked.

"Wow," another added.

"Seeing that would be a trip, Howie."

"Everybody wants to play Hamlet, right? But dying is easy. Comedy is hard, as somebody once said."

The skinny guy who had done the Western voice now did Jerry Lewis in Shakespeare: "Hey lady! To be or not to be, nice lady!"

This time, Howie stayed stone-faced.

"Don't talk against Jerry," he told him. "He's a genius."

There was general, solemn agreement with this. The funny kid slowly withdrew, self-consciously crossing his arms and legs. Howie was efficiently drawing in his acolytes, but he wouldn't let them get too close.

"A genius, like I used to be," he said, quietly, as the lights faded for another act.

I was the only one who heard him. Or who noticed that he was on his third free drink. Even though a new comic was performing, Howie kept muttering to himself. Then he turned and glared at me, with fury in his eyes.

"You're, uh, driving back, right?" I whispered, concerned.

"Look, pal," he mumbled through ice cubes. "Why don't you go find outtakes from *Lassie,* or something?"

I was about to reiterate, indignantly, that TV trivia *wasn't* my specialty, when Howie erupted, ice falling from his mouth.

"I'm not your prisoner, for chrissake!" he whispered-yelled into my ear. "I'm a free man!"

He pushed me to the side, nearly toppling me from my chair. Then, heedless of the luckless person now performing, he started to stumble to the stage.

Seeing him, the whole crowd, of course, went nuts. Ruining the current comic's set, they started chanting "How-ie! How-ie! How-ie!" By the time Howie groped his way under the spotlight—and gently but firmly eased the other guy out of it—I couldn't even hear myself sigh.

Howie waved a grateful hand to stop the crowd. He seemed completely sober now, before them. Maybe I shouldn't have been surprised.

"Don't say I didn't warn you," he said, and the place exploded.

Howie proceeded to perform a carefully constructed act, all of new material, except for a few old comments on toothbrushes. He convulsed the crowd with observations about retirement, children, and sneaking a cigarette away from your wife.

I realized that Howie had never retired; he had been working—"observing"—all along. Like me, he had absolutely no interest in everyday life. Unlike me, he had made a fortune from his alienation. And, after tonight, I knew he would continue to.

He saved his most hilarious material for worthless relatives, freeloaders, and nerds, remarks he delivered looking right at me.

"Let's hear it for him!" Howie yelled. "He's not paying for his meal *tonight,* either!"

Suddenly, with Howie's direction, the spotlight shifted away from the stage. Then it shone, brutally, in my eyes. The crowd whooped and hollered, as I waved, weakly. I thought that Martin Sheen had replaced Harvey Keitel in *Apocalypse Now* and Jodie Foster had done the same for Nicole Kidman in *Panic Room.*

The ring of light moved back to the stage, leaving me blind. Howie began to expound on pocket protectors—what were they really protecting? When I opened my tearing eyes and was able to focus, I saw that the skinny young comic, who had been shot down by Howie, whose face I had never really seen, was leaving the club.

We closed the place. Then I waited with Howie while the garage attendant searched for his car. If he had been pumped after tennis, now he was positively hyper. Howie kept punching and kicking the air, yelling, "I killed! Killed!" More free drinks had returned him to a state of totally loopy inebriation.

When the car arrived, he pushed me away from it.

"I'm not going anywhere with you!" he yelled, sloppily. "You can keep your Jerry Lewis and your . . ." He groped for a word. Then, finally, he invented one: "Your *Clowncried*!"

"Howie—" I tried a reasonable tone, if only to get a lift home at three A.M.

"I'm not going to end up like you!" he spat, barring the car door. "I'm going back to work! I'm bored to goddamn tears! All this . . . retiring . . . is killing me! So here, you want to find that goddamned stupid film—" He counted out a few bills, one of which he stuffed in the attendant's palm. Then he flung the others at me. "Good luck!"

In a minute, he had peeled out, his tires screaming. A baby picture of Howie's son, Elliot, had sailed out at the same time. Now it lay in a puddle on the ground.

I stood there, the money fluttering toward my feet. The attendant only shrugged, looking bemusedly at his windfall: a hundred-dollar bill. Then he left me in the dark garage, alone.

Howie had been giving me more and more power. Finally, he'd allowed me sway over his entire professional life. That was worth a lot more than three hundred bucks, which I now stooped to retrieve. But it was probably the only thing I would ever get from him. I stuffed the dough into my front pants pocket.

I wasn't the only one who wanted the money.

Lurking in the shadows outside, a figure now peeked in from the garage entrance. Then it disappeared. The street was otherwise empty.

I planned to sleep in my own bed that night, which was a few blocks away. I would call Dena first thing in the morning, which was an hour from now.

But first I had to get by the guy outside.

HE WAS ON MY TAIL THE MINUTE I EMERGED ONTO FORTIETH STREET. I heard his footsteps, nearly felt his breath. When I took a quick glimpse behind me, I saw a thin man, his face hidden by a sweatshirt hood.

I cut across Eighth Avenue, at full gallop.

I'd been chased so many times recently, it was almost refreshing to merely get mugged. In a second, I realized that wasn't what was happening.

"Roy!" the guy called, coming after me.

My blood froze, as my feet found the other sidewalk. Without stopping, I looked back again, helplessly, responding to my name. His face was still a black hole beneath his hood. When I turned forward, I was heading right into a mound of garbage at the threshold of an alley.

I tripped and fell onto McDonald's boxes, plastic wrap, Chinese food, and, yes, banana peels. But my friend was conscientious enough to help me up—yanking me by my belt loops and collar and tossing me ahead of him, into the alley.

"Alley oop!"

This wasn't his first time hurting someone; he seemed pretty good at it. I thought about a movie in the early Eighties, *Beginners,* starring Elizabeth McGovern and Keith Gordon as young lovers—a Norman Lear production. It was abandoned, never started up again, and declared dead.

So nearly was I, my face pressed into asphalt. As the man stooped to hammer his fist into my side, I thought of something else. The voice he'd used on "Alley oop!" had been a Homer Simpson imitation. It was almost as good as his Jerry Lewis doing Shakespeare or his cowboy. It was the dismissed young comic.

He punched me again in the side.

"Where is it, Roy?" he said.

What had he said? Before he could speak again—he had already started a syllable—I flailed an elbow back into his throat. My aim was erratic; I hit him in the collarbone, which made my entire arm ring. Still, it shut him up. I took the opportunity to speak.

"Help!"

Amazingly, I was answered by a police siren. Maybe they were napping nearby, I thought. The sound spurred my attacker into flight. As I flipped over, I saw him making for the alley's entrance. His hood hung down, but I could only see the back of his head.

He took a fast left and ran from sight. There was maybe a full minute of siren before the cop car showed, from the other direction. One cop stayed inside while another got out, cautiously. He looked into the alley, where I now sat, nursing my reverberating arm.

"Don't move!"

"Don't worry," I replied.

He wasn't amused. "I said, don't move!"

Wincing, I put my hands up. What else could I do? He had a gun on me. Meanwhile, behind him, in the street, I alone saw a battered white Honda drive by at high speed.

"*What'd* you say you were doing there?"

Same precinct, same detective. Florent stood opposite me again, looking even more the Central Casting cop than before.

"He tried to rob me," I said.

I didn't say that it had to do with *Clown,* even though I figured that it had.

"This have something to do with *The Day the Clown Cried*?" Florent asked.

I closed my eyes, the lids feeling like they weighed a hundred pounds. My luck to always get *this* cop, who thought he was trivial.

"*What?*" I said. "That's the most ridiculous thing I ever heard."

Florent only nodded, with a brief, unconvinced "Uh huh."

"I mean, that's really . . ." I was shaking my head now, clucking with disbelief, "just really crazy . . ."

"Maybe," he shrugged a little. "Maybe."

Before I could start on a new boring trivial discourse—my only line of defense against him, short of crying—Florent had hiked up his pants and left the room.

I rolled my eyes, relieved. Then, with great difficulty, I lifted my bruised body out of the hardwood interrogation chair. There was nothing for the police to hold me on. But maybe I should have asked for their protection.

A few minutes later, on a borrowed cell phone, I called my mother's house. Aunt Ruby told me there'd been no change in Mom's condition. But she'd been secretly ordering more pay-per-view movies—sneaking off again, as it were, to the movies.

"I haven't seen anything in the mail from you," Ruby said, brusquely. "But maybe our mailbox is broken."

Guiltily, I felt in my pocket for the hundreds Howie had chucked at me. I'd have to send the cash in the mail. I hadn't received any more money since Abner's first check.

Speaking of Abner, should I tell him what was going on? I had to let him know where I was headed, after all. But when I called his apartment, his boyfriend answered.

"Abner's in the hospital," Taylor Weinrod told me.

I felt a jolt of panic. Had Stanley Lager struck again? And if so, why?

"It's gout," he explained. "I've been wheeling him around the apartment in a swivel chair."

"Jesus," I said. "I thought only fifteenth-century kings got that."

"Abner always appreciated the past, you know that," Taylor said, indulgently.

I felt even more impatient than ever with Abner's excesses. I left the new address where I could be reached. Then I hung up.

I made one more call. I hoped Dena would pick up Howie's guesthouse phone.

She did.

"I've been so worried," she told me. "Howie came back and told me what happened at the club. Well, he said as much as he could between gropes. He was a little, shall we say, worked up. I didn't mean to hit him that hard. But it's no way to ask a girl to marry you."

"Yeah," I said. "Meeting me apparently gave him new clarity about his own life."

"More than you know. He told me he was coming out of retirement. Then, after I turned down his proposal, he told Luna she'd been paying too much attention to herself and not enough to Elliot. Then he canned me."

"Jeez. That's rough."

"It's okay. Maybe it was time to move on," she said. "You and I will split up. Then reconnoiter."

I explained that the white-faced driver in the Hamptons had followed me to the tennis club and then to the city. I said that, while beating me, he'd asked, "Where is it?" More than that I didn't know.

"Where are you going to go?" I asked.

"I guess to Maine. I have to close up my father's old place. Maybe there'll be more information." She paused, then spoke with real feeling. "I'm sorry it didn't work out with Howie, Roy."

"Well," I said, "let's put it this way. I'm not where I was before."

She took this in.

"Where can I reach you?" she asked. "In New York?"

"No," I replied. "As a matter of fact, in L.A."

After I finished explaining, I handed the cell phone back to its owner. We were standing outside the police station, next to her limo.

Marthe Ludwig, Thor's wife, said she'd wait while I packed my stuff.

PART 3
LOS ANGELES

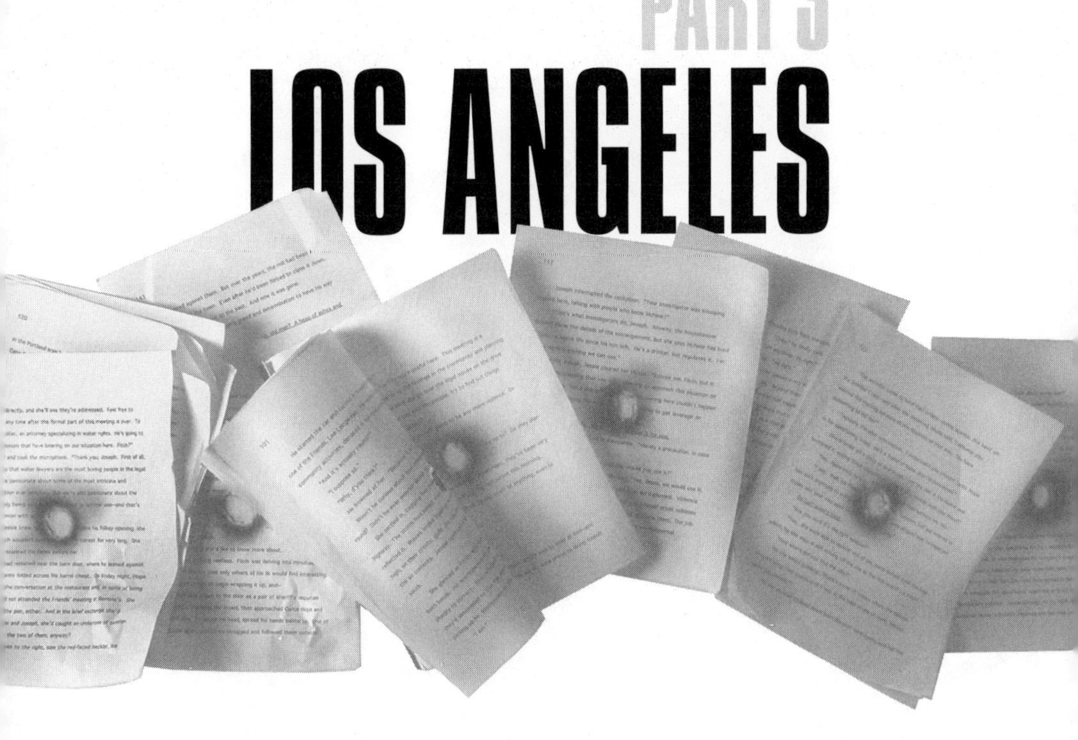

MARTHE HAD ACTUALLY CALLED HOWIE'S HOUSE, LOOKING FOR ME. WHILE she was friendly on our ride to the airport, her manner was also businesslike.

"That *Clown* film," she said. "I checked it up with Howie."

"Did you?" She was decked out in a shiny pantsuit and her big hoop earrings swayed as the limo swerved. Her inexact English was so charming it made me want to cry. I managed to restrain myself.

"It gave me an idea."

"Lots of people would like to own it," I said.

"I don't know about the owning. I am thinking more of Thor."

I followed the thin gold necklaces that cascaded in concentric circles from her neck. They reached the opening of a silk blouse that was virtually unbuttoned. She was as lean as a boy and several inches taller than me, even, it seemed, sitting down. It was all, as the kids say, good.

"Is it about the taxes?" I asked, recalling her husband's problems.

She gave a shrug that meant yes. "Thor needs something now besides the tennis. That's kaput."

"You could have fooled me. I played him."

"Yes. I'm so sorry about that." She seemed sincere, and it appeared that I'd been even more humiliated than I'd thought. "Those shorts, especially."

I only nodded. I knew she represented the height of fashion, in a European pantsuit sort of way. And, suddenly, that made her seem weirdly familiar.

"Weren't you—"

She nodded. "I posed for the perfume. With the ocelot."

A tiny gasp escaped my lips. Marthe had once been the centerpiece of a big ad campaign in print and on TV. She had been photographed in exotic locations with a dangerous animal. How could I not have recognized her? I guessed, after Thor left Gratey McBride, I'd simply stopped following his life.

"But that's over now," she said, quietly. "No more modeling. That's another reason . . . well, that I thought of this."

Being asked to assist a broke sports star and his supermodel wife was high cotton. Still, how would Jerry Lewis come into it?

"This *Clown,* I think," she said, "would make a good vehicle for Thor."

I almost laughed. She wanted Thor Ludwig to be a movie star. The idea was, I'm sure, on many people's minds back in the seventies. Today it seemed a much more dubious proposition.

And a remake of a film that had never even been completed? It was certainly a new concept.

I thought of an aborted eighties film version of Jeffrey Archer's novel *Not a Penny More, Not a Penny Less.* George Segal, Rod Steiger, and George Hamilton had gotten off the plane in Europe to start shooting and found there was no money. It was done later with different actors in 1990 as a TV miniseries.

I told Marthe this, and she was attentive, as always. She was also a bit impatient. So, blushing again, as we reached the airport, I got to a more pertinent concern.

"Who's going to help us find it?" I asked.

"You're going to see," she said, as the driver opened the door.

She kicked my foot a little, with her boot, the same way she had her husband. I watched the chains shift on her chest as she rose.

I knew now this had never been a pure flirtation or even friendship. Someone always needed something and someone else got used. For a trivial man, it was nice to be needed and good to be used. I didn't tell her that someone was willing to kill for the movie. I just let Marthe pull me from my seat with her impossibly warm hand.

Marthe said virtually nothing more on the plane going over. Despite her strapped circumstances, she sprang for first class. Then she took enough pills to sleep, squirmingly, throughout the entire flight. At one point, she flung a silky leg over mine and muttered something sweet. But I knew she was sedated and her eyes covered by a mask.

Restless, I pulled out the book she had placed in the netting of the seat before her. It was the autobiography of the infamous film producer Troy Kevlin, *The Boy-O Keeps Ringing the Bell!* An innovative, jet-set executive in the seventies—producing, among other things, Gratey McBride's Oscar-winning vehicle, *Macaroon Heart*—he'd been derailed by drug charges in the eighties. He couldn't get projects off the ground anymore, and so had written a tell-all memoir. Just as the truth dawned on me, Marthe whispered, her accent even thicker in her sleep,

"Troy will be helping to finding it."

Howie had apparently told Marthe that Troy Kevlin might have information about *Clown*. This was more, of course, than the comic had ever told me; he had just said he met the producer during a tennis match. But I would take my leads where I could get them.

Troy had once lived in Bel-Air, in a famous mansion built by Charlie Chaplin. Now, his circumstances much reduced, he occupied a modest house in Burbank, on a nondescript residential block. With three floors and a backyard, it looked pretty good to me, coming from a one-room walk-up with no counter space.

Marthe put me in a bright room on the ground floor, next to hers and

Thor's. I'd brought my laptop and passport but not Abner's gun. I might need to use the first two things; I didn't want to use the third.

I couldn't see much of the house. I hadn't been to California since I'd pursued *The Magnificent Ambersons,* and the sudden assault of sun made me need to lie down with a cold compress. I had plenty of room on Troy's leather couch, which came from his old mansion and now spanned three quarters of his small living room.

"Can you open your eyes?" Marthe asked, replacing the compress, taking good care of me.

"Not yet," I said, squinting.

This was how Troy and Thor found us: me lying down, Marthe sitting at my side. The two men had walked in from what seemed a long day of shopping. I realized then that the Ludwigs were Troy's permanent houseguests; the couple had lost their own digs to creditors. All three of them had squandered their fortunes, and today the men's bags were from Target, CVS, Subway, and other cost-efficient chains. We were all losers now.

As usual, Thor looked prematurely wizened. He wore a white running suit, his stringy blond hair hit his shoulders, and the sun had turned his face into a pistachio nut.

Beside him, Troy's own skin looked more like the pecan on a praline cookie I had had on the plane. Still lean at sixty-five, he wore a black turtleneck, gray slacks, and a glittery medallion around his neck. His dark sunglasses were the size of dinner plates I'd seen at my mother's house. He was a little piece of seventies Hollywood: a broken piece.

"Here we are," he said, in a gravelly baritone, "the Boy-O and the Strudel."

As I would soon learn, Troy gave tough-guy nicknames to everyone: Strudel referred to Thor's Germanic heritage. Troy himself was, of course, the Boy-O. The habit had started as a charming trait; it became a necessity after a series of small strokes addled Troy's memory. He otherwise seemed unimpaired, frisky, even. Thor was in worse shape.

"Marthe says I played this dude at tennis once," Thor said about me, vaguely, though pleasantly.

"It was just the other day, in New York, sweetie," Marthe said, adjusting my compress, "don't you remember?"

Thor just shrugged, smiled, and didn't respond. Then he reached into his Subway bag, unwrapped a turkey hero and, with two hands, started to eat it, vigorously.

"That's the Strudel," Troy said, watching him. "He wants what he wants when he wants it. First a turkey sandwich, then he takes Poland."

The fifty-year-old joke went down easy for Troy, and he winked at me, as if sharing a hipster's secret. He hobbled over to the couch, showing a little stroke-related stiffness, and shoved in close to Marthe.

"Move over, Legs," he said, fondly.

We were now one big happy family—except for Thor, who sat on a chair opposite, eating and staring off, occasionally making a slight "backhand" gesture.

"I see the setup with *Day the Clown,* and it'll get fannies into seats," Troy said, already planning the remake. "The minute the Spaetzle comes on the screen, dames' hearts will go pitter-pat." Thor had now gone from a dessert to a noodle dish but didn't even know. "We change the plot, of course. Jerry was a clown, Thor will be a tennis player. We'll even get in a little court action."

"In a concentration camp?" I finally opened my eyes, but my head throbbed from more than the light.

"Sure," Troy shrugged. "Vanessa played fiddle in *Playing for Time,* Glenny sang with the choir in *Paradise Road,* Willem made with the fisticuffs in *Triumph of the Spirit.* Don't think I haven't scoped this out."

Apparently he had, researching as many prison camp dramas as he could. How long had Marthe been cooking up this scheme? Since her last tax bill, I figured. I needed to slow this quickly moving train.

"Look," I said, "first we have to actually *find* the film, don't we? Before we can do anything?"

"We'll get it," Troy said, confidently. "We'll be each other's guardian angels, like Clarence in *Wonderful Life.* The one played by . . ." Here he faltered.

"Henry Travers," I said, quickly.

This stopped Troy, and he shot me a look. He clearly had no idea who or, more to the point, what I really was.

"Henry Travers," he said, apparently not wanting to know.

I was beginning to get the sense that Troy believed, given what Marthe may have told him, that this was going to be a slam dunk, to mention another sport I never watched. I knew more than he did.

"Look." I sat up, the compress falling onto my chest. "A man may have died over the movie already. And I've nearly been done in myself—three times."

I felt a hand smelling of almond skin cream start caressing my hair. Then Marthe's lips pressed maternally and meaningfully onto my forehead. It worked: I shut up.

Troy rose, with more spring than I would have expected. He strode from the room. "Piece of cake, Clarence," he shrugged, closing the subject, and was gone.

As I sat there, still seductively muffled, I saw something on the stucco wall Troy had passed. I remembered that William Devane had replaced Roy Thinnes in Hitchcock's last picture, *Family Plot.*

It was a bullet hole. I'd seen enough of them by now to know.

THE NEXT NIGHT WE SAW TROY'S GREATEST HITS.

The dank basement below his kitchen was almost a parody of a screening room, with fold-up chairs, a scuffed Ping-Pong table, and bowls of Paul Newman Popcorn. Troy ran videos on a giant TV screen, and provided partly informative but mostly intrusive commentary.

"I had to arm wrestle Zanuck for that setup," he'd say, about a complex location, or "[Some forgotten actress] and I were ships in the night. She was a great lady."

His movies from the Seventies had been, admittedly, superb. For a brief and shining moment, he had used his savvy to complete a few classics, before drug arrests laid him low. The films still looked good, what I could stay awake to watch, through my jet lag.

He saved the best for last.

"This is my baby," he said. "One from the *Macaroon Heart*."

And that was what it was: The comedy of hustlers and grifters that had earned Thor's ex-wife her Oscar. Playing her father figure, Gratey's co-star was fiery German actor Graus Menzies. After two hours of machinations, she learns that Graus is her *actual* father.

"There's the Lollipop," Troy said, when Gratey's six-year-old self came on. "Don't believe the gossip. A dwarf didn't dub her. I coached her every line myself."

There was no mention of her collapse in adulthood, how she had been found wandering, stoned, clutching her award, in a low-rent neighborhood of L.A. There was no mention, either, of where she was now; no one seemed to know.

I had always thought the movie treacly and slept through most of it tonight. I was awakened by what sounded like goats mating. I turned and saw Troy and Thor crying, hoarsely and helplessly, mourning younger days, better movies, early marriages, and more money.

Sitting behind me, Marthe was conspicuously dry-eyed. During the movie, downing Bloody Marys, she had playfully tossed pieces of popcorn at my head whenever it drooped. She had also done that boot-kicking thing to the back of my chair.

"Kitsch," she said afterward, in her Dietrich way. Then she launched into a long, quiet, cranky monologue in German, the only words of which I recognized were *Gratey* and *sheiss*. There were clearly old wounds here that I couldn't understand.

Sniffling, Troy was soon on his feet, pacing before the now-dark TV, acting out his future plans.

"I can see it now . . ." He made that two-hand framing gesture. "With Thor in *Day the Clown,* I'll be back in the game, the Boy-O ringing the bell . . ."

His future star was huddled in his chair, still bawling. Marthe now knelt beside her husband, and cradled his head on her shoulder. She whispered deeply into his ear, half in German, half in English. This time, I heard and understood a bit more.

"Don't worry . . ." I picked up. "This is going to be it. . . . Just trust me . . . Trust me . . ."

Marthe carried a lot on her slight shoulders; she was certainly carrying *this* ball by herself. I felt a slight chill, thinking of how much seemed at stake.

Actually, the chill was coming from the basement door. Troy had left it open after climbing the cement steps.

A few minutes later, from upstairs, I heard the doorbell.

There was a pause. Then, above us, what I assumed were Troy's feet walked slowly to answer it. There were muffled voices, and a barely audible cry. Then I heard the front door unmistakably slam.

I turned, concerned, to look at Marthe. Thor's blubbering had subsided, and he had fallen asleep. She glanced up, caught my questioning look, and immediately avoided it.

"What's going—" I started to ask, but never finished. Other, worse sounds had started to come through the floor.

Feet were pursuing other feet. There was a loud thump overhead, like someone falling, which shook the basement.

"Hey!" I said, sitting up. I got no help from Marthe. She was busy groping in her bag for a diversionary smoke.

More disturbing noises began. It sounded like someone being pushed into a cabinet. Plates fell and smashed.

I stood and ran to the staircase. Above me, the door was open but a crack. By the time I'd placed a foot on the first step, it was pushed shut and crudely locked.

Now the chill I felt had nothing to do with the weather. I flew up the stairs and started pounding on the door.

"Hey!" I said again, this time to those I couldn't see.

I placed my ear against the wooden door. I thought I heard someone say "a warning," and Troy's gravelly voice reply, using the archaic phrase "moolah." Then I heard a hand slap a face.

I started pounding on the door.

"Let us out!" I yelled, my voice cracking. I looked back down at Marthe. She was idly kicking her boot, smoking her cigarette, her husband's sleeping head in her lap.

"What the *hell* is going on?" I called down to her.

She shrugged. "Troy's business."

"What?"

"I say, just wait," she said, louder. "It will be over soon."

Not soon enough. I pressed my ear again to the door and once more pounded, futilely. I perceived more muted mayhem. Troy contemptuously muttered "gat," tough-guy for *gun*. Hand made contact a last time with face, this time hard. Feet walked across floor. Then the front door was opened and this time quietly closed.

My jet lag ended by dismay, I recalled that Betty Hutton had replaced Judy Garland in *Annie Get Your Gun*.

"Hey!"

As in a comedy routine, I was now knocking on air, as the door flew swiftly open. I stumbled into the kitchen. Its tiled floors were littered with the remains of china.

Troy, who had let me out, was walking quickly away, his back to me. I saw that he was pressing a dish towel to the side of his face. The freezer hung open. An empty ice tray was in the sink.

"Are you all right?" I called after him.

"Fit as a fiddle. Thanks for asking," he muttered, through cloth. "No man is a failure when he has friends."

He walked, quickly this time, to stairs leading up. The cliché from *It's a Wonderful Life* hung in the air like a moldy smell.

I moved to a window of the house and pulled aside its curtain. I saw a car peeling away from the curb. It wasn't the dinged-up Honda of *my* nemesis, that was for sure. It was a fancy Mercedes.

Troy, I knew now, had problems of his own.

MY PROBLEMS, THOUGH, WERE ABOUT TO BE SOLVED. THE PHONE WAS RINGing, and I answered it.

"Good news," Dena said, out-of-breath. "I got the film."

"What? That's fantastic!"

"The bad news is . . . I can't watch it."

I stopped for a second, not sure what she meant. Then, carrying the cordless, I shut the door in my ground-floor guest room. "Slow down and back up."

"I went through everything in my father's place here, in Bar Harbor. It wasn't easy. He seemed never to have thrown anything away. But at the bottom of one drawer seemed to be his most private things. Bank books, emergency phone numbers, porn magazines, more pictures of me."

"Sweet."

"And, wrapped in a plastic bag, was a videotape."

"So. He's had it for a while."

"Looks that way."

Under my door, I saw a light going on and off in the hall. Then I heard footsteps so light they could only have been Marthe's. I lowered my voice further.

"This comes at a good time."

"What? I can't hear you."

"I said, this comes at a good time. I'm pretty sure things aren't kosher here."

"Well, it *is* L.A."

Spoken like a true trivial person, I thought; maybe there was hope for Dena yet. I realized suddenly, caught in this house of has-beens and half-perceived truths, that I missed her. I also realized something else.

"How do you know it's *Clown*? Was there a label or something?"

"You mean, one that says 'Priceless Unreleased Film'? Roy, that's beneath you."

Dena was taking a mean mother tone. I didn't miss her so much now. Still, I thought my question was valid.

"The fact is, you don't know. It could be more porn, may your father, uh, rest in peace. Why can't you watch it?"

"I don't know how to work the VCR. It's an old one, anyway. His apartment's sort of a dump, to be honest. And, sadly enough, I think it belongs to me now. I don't know the New England real estate market well enough to—"

"Look, I don't mean to interrupt—" I heard footsteps from the room next to mine. The wall was creaking. Was someone leaning against it, listening? "But how are we going to know for sure?"

"Well, you'll watch it out there. I mailed it to you."

"Here?"

"Don't worry. I FedExed it."

I didn't know why it seemed like a lousy idea, but it did. Something told me it wasn't safe to have Troy Kevlin anywhere near the film. Besides, what if it got lost? There were trivial cops; maybe there were trivial mailmen.

"I put it to your attention, Roy, don't worry."

For all her common sense and competence, Dena still lacked the essential irrational paranoid quality that distinguished the trivial. I liked her and hated her for it. Regardless, it was too late to do anything but wait.

"When I get it, I'm going home. Even Abner is better than this." I surprised myself, saying it. But as my wall creaked again, I began to prefer the devil I knew.

"Keep me posted," Dena said, warmly.

"I will."

Neither of us spoke then. Between Dena's father and my mother, I supposed we were filling in as family for each other. Maybe that would explain the awkwardness about everything else. It also explained why, when I hung up, I felt alone. And a little afraid.

I tiptoed out of my room, carrying my toiletries. I looked to the left, saw the bathroom. I looked to the right, saw the room next to mine.

The door was open a bit. The light was on, and I heard strange, shifting movements. Then I heard a woman's voice.

"Roy?" Marthe called.

I cursed, silently. A little earlier, I would have welcomed more contact with her. Now I dreaded it. Things change—and faster in L.A.

"Yes?" I said.

She didn't answer. I had no choice but to enter the room.

Marthe was indeed alone. She was lying on her back in the middle of the floor. She wore only a leotard, and her long brown legs were sticking straight up in the air. She brought them down slowly over her shoulders. Then she rested her knees on the yoga mat beneath her.

"I'll be right with you," she said.

I sat in a chair, as she breathed in and out, meditatively, curled in her half-circle. I tried not to stare, to respect the contemplative nature of her activity, but soon simply had to. The backs of Marthe's perfectly shaped thighs, covered in black tights, rounded near her ears, were too compelling.

"Do you mind my doing this?" she asked, moving slowly back to a seated position.

"Not at all," I replied.

"I have to. Otherwise my sciatica is too bad."

I nodded, as Marthe tucked one leg beneath herself and stretched the other.

"This is why I quit modeling," she said.

She pointed her toes, an activity I had never thought erotic before. She grunted, as she gripped the ankles of her elongated leg. Then she looked over at me, her face glistening with sweat.

"There's a terrible pain in standing still."

The comment seemed to have a hidden meaning. Her glance had a not-so-hidden one. I was meant to leave my chair and join her. Trying to avoid the terrible, entrancing power of her gaze—one she'd perfected in that shoot with the ocelot, I thought—I had to turn away.

"Look," I said, "I don't know how much longer I'll be here."

"What?" Marthe had just switched tucked and untucked legs.

I didn't want to mention that *Clown* might be headed my way; why whet her appetite, and what if it weren't true? I also wished to be discreet about our host.

"Troy's into bad people for something. I think he may need me a lot more than I need him."

As if on cue, there was a sound from upstairs. A door creaked open. I heard a man's voice. And, unless I was crazy, a woman's.

I was about to ask if Troy had company—so soon after being beaten, he was in better shape than I thought. But Marthe spoke before I could.

"He's not the one who needs you," she said.

She had me; I looked her way. Marthe was sitting up, her feet splayed apart, like a rag doll or a child. One of her hands was extended to me, the fingers trembling. She looked gauche; to be more accurate, she looked painfully human.

The noises from upstairs grew louder, then softer, then stopped. I rose from the chair and flew to her, like the female vampires in *Dracula*. Director Tod Browning had meant to make the film with Lon Chaney, but the actor died. So he cast Bela Lugosi.

"Tell me something," she said, as I joined her on the mat.

"What?"

"Tell me something I don't know."

I looked into Marthe's eyes, which were glistening with interest. I knew suddenly what she wished for me to say.

"Marlon Brando," I said, "replaced Montgomery Clift in *Reflections in a Golden Eye*."

Marthe nodded, breathing deeply, and not in the yoga way. Then she blinked, very slowly, asking me to go on.

"Robert Mitchum replaced Burt Lancaster in *Maria's Lovers*."

Her breath came quicker. Marthe took down one strap of the leotard, then the other. She slowly pulled the garment to her waist. She'd been naked with the ocelot, too, and younger, but she'd never been more beautiful.

For the first time in my life, trivia was someone else's aphrodisiac. She didn't meet so much, as she'd said, the nerd.

"Go on," she said.

"And . . ."

I racked my brain. The only problem was: I couldn't remember a single other fact.

It didn't matter. Marthe had laid down on the mat and pulled me to her.

"Just watch out for my legs," she said. "They're killing me."

I promised to be careful. I hadn't been with anyone since my *Ambersons* adventure. Marthe didn't need to know that, though I sensed she would have understood. What she was doing was partly from opportunism—she wanted the movie, after all—but it was partly from desire, too. Thor could hardly raise his racket now.

No matter what I'd intended when I came in, I wasn't going anywhere, not anymore. If that made me a schmuck, I had been called worse things.

"My film greek," she murmured.

"Geek," I whispered back.

She took the information in.

"Geek," she repeated, unless I closed her mouth gently with my own.

Soon I didn't care about the noises coming from upstairs.

"WHAT DO YOU MEAN, YOU'RE STAYING?" DENA ASKED, THE NEXT DAY.

I found myself stammering, trying to sound resolute. "Just for a while. I think I can . . . you know, use things here to my advantage."

There was a long pause on the other end of the line. A morning shower had failed to remove Marthe's scent from me, and I closed my eyes, inhaling it.

"Well, okay," Dena said, unsurely, "if you think it's safe."

It was, of course, unsafe. Especially considering what I now held in my hands: the Federal Express package. I was lucky it had arrived before any of my dissolute friends had gotten up.

"I'm too jazzed to even open it," I said.

"I know how you feel." It seemed Dena was being infected by the *Clown* disease, too. "Just be careful with it."

"Believe me, I will."

There was a longer pause. Then Dena's tone changed once again to the unpleasantly maternal. "I sent it to you, Roy, because you're the most knowledgeable—and trustworthy—person about this subject that I know.

But if there's something else going on in L.A. now . . . I wish you'd tell me."

I sighed. I could have just fled with the tape back to New York, to familiar sources and surroundings. But I had lied to myself that there was no harm in remaining. And then I lied to Dena.

"There's no harm in remaining," I said.

All I could think about was the way Marthe had kicked away her leotard, sending it upon the bed we hadn't used. I could still see vague fissures from the yoga mat on my legs, arms, and back. It was a minute before I remembered that I might have *The Day the Clown Cried.* And that surprised even me.

Of course, who knew whether I had it? The ragged, banged-up tape, once I opened the bag and saw it, could have been anything. It was as much a relic as my Hollywood friends, and about as poorly preserved.

I e-mailed Abner that I might have *Clown*. Then, after leaving an elliptical note for Marthe, I walked up to the nearest thoroughfare—Olive Avenue, it turned out—and called a cab from a pay phone in a mini-mall.

When the driver heard where I was headed—"Santa Monica, please"—he smiled, bemused. Taking a rube on a lengthy trip in bumper-to-bumper traffic would pad his pocket nicely. But I didn't feel safe watching it in Troy's house. I clutched the tape as tightly as I would my child, as I made my way to check it out.

The promenade in Santa Monica was home to any number of overpriced restaurants and gift shops. I moved uneasily among the tubby tourists and emaciated homeless who mingled on the mall like two competing occupying armies.

I was trying to find an independent video store that catered to the college crowd. I intended to consult a trivial man I heard worked as a clerk there, having just been thrown out of UCLA. A trivial boy, I should say: Kent Moreno was only thirteen. He had lied about his age to get the job.

I found him atop a ladder in The Video Hole, rearranging gift DVDs of Buster Keaton silents. The mailbag with the tape was jammed into my armpit like a block of gold.

"What you got there, Roy?" said a voice with a faint Puerto Rican accent.

I wasn't aware Kent was even looking down at me. But he, despite his age—and string-bean shape, which made him look even younger—always seemed to know everything. That accounted for his early college admission and, it appeared, his early dismissal.

"I'll let you know in a minute," I said.

He scampered down the rungs, his braces reflecting in the harsh store light. His red Keds hit the floor with a thud.

"That a gift for me?"

"Hardly. I need a favor."

"What's in it for Kent?"

I paused, not even having considered reciprocation. Then, thinking fast, I offered him something I had no idea I could get. "Gratey McBride's autograph."

Kent stopped in his tracks. I knew that the precocious lad identified heavily with her similar role in *Macaroon Heart*. I also knew that neither Troy nor Thor nor Marthe had a clue as to where the poor soul was.

"Sold, she's my girl," he said, surprised. "If you're not shoveling coal, that is."

"I'm not, I'm for real," I lied. "I'll also throw in—" And here I named a figure—smaller than if I hadn't promised him anything, and pretty much all I had left from Abner.

"Cool."

"Now, I need someplace safe to watch a tape."

Kent gave an intrigued look at the tape I was slowly revealing. Then he was diverted by a customer at the desk.

"Hey, don't rent that!" he yelled, pointing to the teen comedy the guy was holding. "It sucks! Rent something good!"

I smiled a little and shook my head. Kent wouldn't last much longer at work than he did at school, I figured. The customer sheepishly returned his tacky choice, and the kid checked out my goods again.

"What is it, *Ambersons*? Oh, sorry, I heard you already found that. It must be *Clown* then."

Kent was only kidding, suggesting the least plausible possibility, but I was a little rattled nonetheless. I tried to appear unruffled.

"Right, *Clown,*" I said.

"Did you know Jerry's first film without Dean, *The Delicate Delinquent,* was supposed to have been a Martin and Lewis picture? But instead—"

"Darren McGavin played Dean's part. Don't mess."

Like any preteen worth his salt, Kent liked yanking his elders' chains. He wasn't used to being yanked back. So now he bowed, broadly and embarrassingly, in deference to me.

"There's only one thing," I said. "You can't watch with me. If you do, no Gratey and no dough. Understood?"

"Oh, I get it. It's footage of you and some chick, back in . . ." he looked at the ancient tape, "precable times." Kent made what he thought was a hand gesture, signifying sex. For all his attitude, he was still thirteen, and it looked like he was milking a fly. "Relax. I won't peek."

I was about to hand him the tape and a small down payment. But Kent started haranguing another customer.

"Hey, you! I told you guys, you can't come in here! Now beat it!"

It wasn't a tourist in loud shorts, like the last time. It was one of his competitors for Promenade space: a homeless man. He was young, thin, and unkempt, with a matted black beard and long and stringy hair that hid his face. Turning away, swiftly, he grunted, offended.

But he didn't leave.

"I said," Kent yelled, "get lost!"

"Look," I said, "I don't have much time, so—"

Kent was oblivious; he was too busy marching to the man. Stopping before him, he looked his most childish as he tried to be most tough.

"This is a place of—"

The man shot out a dirty hand and grabbed hold of Kent's collar. Before I knew what was happening, he had lifted him by his *Plan 9 from Outer Space* T-shirt and tossed him right into the nearest wall of tapes. Kent smashed into a shelf of GUILTY PLEASURES and dropped like a scrawny doll onto the floor.

Then the man turned slowly toward me.

I LOOKED AROUND. OUTSIDE THE STORE, THE WHOLE WORLD SEEMED TO BE passing by. Inside, there was just the three of us.

"Hey!" I said, as I always seemed to.

I meant to advance; instead I backed away. The guy was coming for me, throwing his arms around, smashing whatever was in his path. A *Twilight Zone* box set flew and fell, deafeningly. The head of a Jim Carrey cutout was severed. A mobile of Mickey Mouse was yanked from the ceiling and stomped.

I was next in line.

My allegiances were confused: Should I save Kent, myself, or the tape? The decision was not made by me. Springing from the floor with the resilience of youth, Kent came barreling toward the guy from behind. The guy, for his part, reached out and took hold of my tape.

"Hey!"

The man and I had a tug-of-war for the prize; he bested me with one great yank. At the same time, he turned and caught the advancing kid with an elbow to the sternum. Kent went down a second time. Then, stuffing the VHS beneath his dirty shirt, the homeless man made for the front door.

I shot after him, stepping over my younger pal.

"Sorry," I said.

"No problem," Kent replied, and got up again, without missing a beat.

The two of us motored after the man, who was not, as I now knew, what he seemed to be.

"That's some strange homeless dude," Kent commented.

"Tell me about it."

How had he found me? Car driver. Clown face. Comic. Now homeless man. On both coasts, whatever part he played, he always had the same objective: to get the film and then kill me.

Pushing more tapes to the floor—comedies, classics, he smashed every genre—the man broke out of the place. The little welcoming bell on the door chimed, stupidly, for him and then us.

The guy wasn't impressed by the crowd on the mall. He ran into and through them, sideswiping tourists and other vagrants, like a ferocious football star. I had a hard time keeping up, brushed aside by shopping bags (tourists) and shopping carts (vagrants). His dirty dark head was now almost lost to my sight.

"Get on his other side!" I heard someone cry.

When I turned to the voice, I saw Kent, who seemed to be literally flying by. Glancing down, I saw his Keds perched expertly upon a skateboard, which, I hadn't even noticed, he had grabbed on our way out of the store.

Now I was running to keep up with *him*. I was coughing out air, as Kent barely breathed; between thirteen and thirty-six, there was a world of changes. Maintaining this pace, we closed in on our prey.

"Get on his other side!" he yelled again.

Now I sort of understood. Weaving in and out of the mall packed with people, I reached the "homeless" guy's left, as Kent closed in on his right. The boy rode the board, knees bent, arms balancing, as if catching a giant wave. He waited, just waited, for his chance.

There was the briefest of breaks in the mob. Then Kent took his shot.

Swerving the board with an audible squeal of wheels, he rushed toward the guy. Seeming not to stop, he grabbed harshly at the man's midsection. Shouting words no thirteen-year-old should know, Kent freed the tape from where the man held and hid it.

Then he chucked it to me.

We were all football stars now. Though I had never played in my life, I caught the toss like a hall of famer. Cradling it close to my gut, head bent, I ran shockingly fast, wiggling in and out of the Promenade throng.

When I checked back behind me, I saw Kent zoom away, his feet hidden, moving as adroitly as a Foosball figure. He shot me one last wave before returning to the job he was bound to lose.

The bad guy now headed for me.

PANTING, I BROKE FROM THE PROMENADE, ONTO SURROUNDING COMMERCIAL streets. I powered past stores and parking garages toward the scent of water.

In the Hamptons, it meant a dead end. Here, it signaled freedom.

I reached a huge thoroughfare, where gaudy hotels lined the block. Past it was a highway, with mad traffic going either way. Beyond that was a grassy area filled with sightseeing chairs and camps of homeless families. After that: the Pacific Ocean.

The safest route was to flee into a hotel, pretend I was a guest, and hope my friend, in his unseemly new disguise, would not dare enter. The riskiest way was into traffic, which resembled the ocean in the endless relentlessness of its oncoming cars.

I snapped a look over my shoulder. The guy was coming, his need seeming only to give him energy.

I ran right onto the highway. The PCH, I think they call it.

Drivers honked and screamed; tires swerved all around. I never stopped as I danced through cars coming north and south. Feeling exhaust fumes at my feet, bumpers inches from my flesh, I kept my eyes locked upon the beach ahead. It drew me as it had the other losers who had come there to live outdoors.

"Lunatic!" people screamed, and other things less flattering.

Not even Jim Brown ran the gauntlet as well in *The Dirty Dozen*. His co-star in that film, John Cassavetes, replaced Andrew Bergman as director of 1986's *Big Trouble*.

My feet landed on the other curb with the finality of a winning marathon runner's. I turned and saw the massive road I had traversed. The side from which I'd started was so far away, I couldn't tell if my enemy remained there. Carrying my tape, I headed for a rest, to the plastic chairs placed just yards away.

I never reached them.

A shattering pain landed on my shoulders and back. A second later, my face was pressing grass and concrete, my body prone upon the ground. A chair was bouncing away, having served its purpose as a weapon.

I lifted my throbbing head and turned my neck, which rang with agony. I saw a gang of homeless men restraining my chameleon pal. He had made it across, after all—before me. He fought to be released, cursing and shouting.

"Let me go, you sons of bitches!"

Fortunately, they didn't.

The tape was underneath me, still held improbably in my hands. I stood up with it, groggily, moving more like a former quarterback on old-timer's day.

I heard the wail of an oncoming siren. I stumbled to the nearest corner, which I turned. The safest place to go was back to Troy Kevlin's house. And that was a pretty sad statement.

I HAD RUN OUT OF MONEY FOR A RETURN CAB RIDE AND HAD TO CALL FOR A lift. To my surprise, Troy picked me up personally. He said he was coming to the neighborhood anyway.

"There was a sale on socks at Filene's," he explained.

Sure enough, bags of the gold-toed kind filled the back of his shabby Volvo. There was also a box from Domino's Pizza, with a half-eaten pie inside.

He didn't even notice my condition; my face was as red as a pepper and my hair was standing on end. Maybe he was used to people looking roughed-up; his own scars were healing under Band-Aids. How Troy saw *anything* through his huge dark glasses, I had no idea. But he maneuvered the car adequately, all the while colorfully narrating events of his past, present, and future.

"I just dropped off Captain Von Trapp," he said, using one more nickname for Thor. "He's got another charity match."

Then we drove in silence for a while.

"We need some laughs," he said, suddenly.

"What do you mean?"

"In *Day the Clown*. Dying is easy. Comedy is hard. Maybe Jerry forgot that."

Politely, I didn't respond.

"What do you think of Romy?" he asked.

"Romy?"

"Schneider. We'll give Thor a g.f., add a little leg."

G.f. meant girlfriend; I knew that much from *Variety*. I paused, then proceeded, carefully. "She's dead, isn't she? Romy Schneider?"

Troy pursed his lips a second, then recovered. "She was a great kid."

We rode in a more respectful silence now. Troy's comments made the whole notion of the remake seem more dubious than ever. I thought this was a good time to broach a key subject. I tried to sound casual.

"So where's the money coming from?"

"Say again?"

"The funding. You know. For the remake."

Troy was disturbingly silent now. I sensed tension, even hostility, beneath his bonhomie.

"Well . . . I'll know when I get the flick."

Now I saw another side to him, the hard-nosed negotiator who had once made decent films. But what were we haggling over?

"And when do you think that will be?" I moved the big tape now, hiding it beneath my leg. "You got a timeline?"

I was talking Troy's lingo now—dated tough-guy—and he clearly liked the interplay.

"Cards on the table?" he asked.

"Sure."

"I called Jerry about it, but he hasn't called back."

Why was I not surprised? He hadn't called Howie; he never talked to anyone about it.

"So I'm depending on *you*."

He glanced at me, pointedly. I nodded, slowly. What he meant, of course, was: No matter what he'd promised Marthe, he had no intention of making a movie with Thor as the star.

Troy owed dangerous people lots of money. The coveted *Clown* would be worth lots. And *I* was going to help him get it.

I felt a bit faint. Here was another nauseating motive for finding the film. The impulse to go back to New York was never greater. Yet I could still feel Marthe's fingers curling, luxuriously, around my neck. I bet she knew nothing of Troy's real intentions.

"Now you tell *me* . . ." Troy made the final turn, heading back to his house.

"Yes?"

"What's that tape you got there?"

I shouldn't have been surprised he'd seen it. The thing was the size of a goiter, and it was underneath my thigh. I decided to imitate the attitude of my fearless young friend, Kent.

"It's *Clown,*" I said. "Of course."

"Funny," he said, and took the bait.

I was off the hook. For now.

I couldn't help noticing other acquisitions in the back of Troy's car. Next to the socks were enough bandages to wrap a mummy. And a container of what looked like syringes. For whom? I didn't think Troy had backslid into drugs. But I didn't ask.

"Nothing happened," I told Marthe that night. "I'm fine."

I had thought long and hard about telling her the truth. We were, after all, moving upon her yoga mat again. But instead I steeled myself against trusting her. I had placed the tape deep in my luggage and stashed it beneath my bed.

"But so many nicks and bruises," she said, deliciously examining every one.

"I just fell down. They say nobody walks in L.A. And now I've found out why."

It was a ridiculous thing to say, though no more so than "I was seeing the sights" about why I'd gone to Santa Monica. But it would have to do for now. I knew that she and her host had different agendas, neither one to my benefit.

Marthe wanted another thing, too: to stop me from listening to the sounds upstairs. Nothing against myself, I didn't think passion kept her clutching my ears as male and female voices drifted through the ceiling.

"Who *is* that?" I couldn't ignore the moving and talking overhead.

"Shh . . ."

A second-floor door opened, then shut. Through Marthe's pressing palms, I heard what could only be Troy's feet slipping, stiffly, down the stairs. He was cursing to himself, quietly, like Popeye.

Then there was a knock at Marthe's door.

"Legs!" Troy called. "Company's almost here! Come on, Arm Candy, put a motor on it!"

Marthe's hands fell away, slowly. One finger remained at my lips. She called back, weakly, "I'll be right there."

"Where's the Angel?" He meant me.

Marthe's finger pressed a bit harder. "I don't see him."

"Well, if you do, tell him to make an appearance."

There was a pause. Then Troy walked away, cursing again.

Something was about to happen, and I had a strange feeling it wouldn't be pretty.

"Maybe you don't want to be here right now," she whispered.

But it was too late: The front doorbell was ringing.

TROY WAS HAVING A SHINDIG.

Coming through the door were eight or ten of the hottest young male directors in Hollywood. I recognized Lucas Mallomill, a white guy who made faux Hong Kong action films, and Alan Boilerman, who made quirky comedies about dysfunctional families. Most were dressed in indie style—backward caps, flannel shirts—and all arrived as if to a frat party, carrying six-packs of beer, bags of chips, and a raucous 'tude.

"Boy-O!"

This wasn't their first time at the house. They greeted the older man as they might a reprobate uncle, giving him soul handshakes and pats on the back.

"What's cooking?" one of them asked, retro-beatnik-style.

"Only spaghetti, and that ain't ready," Troy answered, not missing a beat.

"Hey, where're the chicks?" another wondered.

"That's my Amish," Troy used a nickname, chucking the fellow's chin beard. "We got what you want, don't worry."

I had left Marthe's room and was standing at the back of the crowd. I noticed four women in the living room. They were blondes wearing short glittery dresses and had obviously been surgically enhanced. They waited, patiently, one checking makeup, another her watch. The young men were clearly there to partake in Troy's Seventies-style fun, which was discouraged in their politically correct age. Thor wandered through the room like a ghost. Marthe was still hiding in her room.

Troy rattled off as many nicknames as he could recall—from Lox Spread to Der Bingle to Shemp—but by his last guest he had wearied. The guy, skinny and bearded, apparently unknown to him, got only Director, which was more a description than a sobriquet.

"And this . . ." he said, at last, approaching me, "is my newest pal." I sensed Troy squinting at me behind his huge shades. The best he could come up with was "Clarence Travers," mixing up the *Wonderful Life* actor with his role.

The others nodded at me, politely, correctly sensing I wasn't on the A-list. Seeing their mixed reaction, Troy felt obliged to explain. He made the gesture meaning money, rubbing his thumb and first two fingers.

"He's providing a bell for me to ring," he said, and winked.

Since the *Clown* adventure began, from Abner to Howie to Troy, I had been cast in lots of different roles. A sugar daddy seemed the least likely. I saw polite skepticism on the young directors' faces.

Clearly, Troy thought this gathering would have networking potential for him. But his guests were, to put it politely, there for their own reasons.

"We should work together," I heard Troy say to Lucas Mallomill.

"That's what we're doing now," the Hong Kong wannabe replied, clearly yearning to approach the rented girls.

Troy held him there, and whispered something in the young man's ear. But Mallomill only shrugged, impatiently, saying, "I'm not holding. Ask someone else."

Then he escaped, leaving Troy looking bereft.

His house, however, looked flush. There were jars of fancy imported olives, expensive fresh cheeses, even a tin of caviar. Champagne bottles sat in ice buckets. It was nothing like the cheap fare that he and his tenants normally consumed. (Last night: Sloppy Joe's.)

Now his guests obliviously scarfed down the fancy food as they jostled for space next to the women. The large-screen TV had been moved up from the basement; raunchy hip-hop music videos ran on it; some men boogied down with the babes, banging into furniture. Others disappeared into rooms with them. Troy was being treated like a doorman; few did more than glance at him before taking more advantage of his hospitality.

I would have felt sorry for the Boy-O if he hadn't cast me in a role that exploited me. And if I hadn't suddenly sensed that this role put me in danger.

One guest hung back, close to the front door. He was different from the other men: older, more subdued, less casually dressed. About forty, he wore a dark suit and his hair was carefully moussed and combed. Troy seemed genuinely surprised to see him. He even removed his glasses and nervously rubbed his deeply ringed eyes.

"I didn't expect you," he said.

"Surprise," the man replied.

"Do you want some chow? Some bubbly? A lap dance, maybe?"

The man shook his head very, very slowly.

"That's not why I came," he said. "And you know it."

I recognized the guy's voice. I had heard it when I had eavesdropped, while locked in the basement. He was the one who'd slapped Troy's face.

"Just give me a little bit more time."

"You've had more than enough."

"Okay, okay," Troy said, rattled. "Let me introduce you to someone."

To my horror, he started approaching me.

"Clarence?" he said.

I fled, walking swiftly toward the other guests. I found myself bumping into Lucas Mallomill, who was trying to show a befuddled Thor some kung fu moves. The first guy didn't acknowledge me; the second didn't remember.

With Troy and the thug at my back, I headed next for Alan Boilerman.

He stood—shyly, I noticed—over a plate of shrimp toast. I quickly acted as if he and I had met before.

"Hey, Alan," I said. "How's it going?"

The director was dressed in what can only be called nerd chic—big glasses, stiff dress jacket over pressed white shirt and chinos. It was a postmodern comment on being trivial, different from the real thing. He tried to be polite.

"Do we . . . have we met?" he asked.

I was sweating now. "Sure, you know. Roy Milano. From the Fest."

This seemed like an all-purpose description, and, to my surprise, it worked.

"Oh," he said. "Sure, sure. How's it going?"

"Just great," I said, taking him by the shoulder and maneuvering him farther into the house. "Look . . . I, uh, was just wondering what you're up to. Another quirky family comedy?"

I hoped the description wasn't too caustic; his work was way too twee for me. Luckily, the subject of himself engrossed Boilerman, and he opened up. "No, actually. I'm going to try a stretch next."

"Is that right? How so?" I wiped my wet brow.

"I'm going to direct *The Seven Ordeals of Quelman*."

I stopped, even though I meant to keep going. "You're kidding."

"No. I just heard yesterday. Do you know the books? It's going to be a real monster project, a whole series of films, starting with . . ."

I pretended to listen, the film plan being known to me. We had reached a dark hallway, away from the party proper. When I glanced back, I saw that Troy's friend had been intercepted by one of the girls. She was standing very close to him, her rock-hard breasts pressed against his suit. I breathed a little easier, turning back to Alan.

"Who's going to adapt it?" I asked, knowing full well.

"I am, actually," Alan said, adjusting his horn-rimmed glasses. "I mean, they had a writer on it. But it was, you know, awful stuff. So I told them I would only do it if I could do my own scripts. I'm going to start from scratch."

I was dumbfounded. "Good for you."

Thoughts were swirling around my head, none of them pleasant. If Abner was off the project—he probably didn't even know it yet—that meant no more money would be forthcoming from him. How would I even get home?

I glanced back. Roughly, Troy's friend shook off the attentions of the overbuilt blonde. Then he was on the move again, and coming my way.

"Well, good luck with that," I said, quickly, to Alan.

"What? Oh, uh, thanks. So what are *you*—"

It would have been nice to schmooze more; Boilerman seemed relatively unaffected. But I would have to take a rain check. I was too busy trying not to get killed.

Soon, so was everyone else. I heard a gun go off.

TROY'S HOUSE GOT ANOTHER WOUND IN ITS WALL.

The bullet—real this time, I knew instinctively—rocketed into the stucco in the hall, not far from my head. Plaster flew into the air like confetti. Alan Boilerman dropped immediately to the floor, whether in a defensive measure or a faint, I didn't know.

I looked up. I saw that the crowd in the living room was scrambling for its life, food, booze, and boobs flying. This was no Hong Kong action movie; this was the worst of reality.

Standing in the center of them, undeterred, was the guy who wanted his dough. He was pointing his gun. He wasn't aiming at me. After all, I was in the shadows of the hall, pressed against the smoking wall. He was aiming at Troy, who was right in front of him, running in a crouch, as if the gun had begun a race.

Troy managed to rigidly round a corner, passing me and the fallen Boilerman, as a second shot peeled out. Again, the wall above me exploded. The former big shot had just managed to escape with his life.

Then I felt someone pull me by the hand.

"Come on!" he said.

I was yanked down another hallway and through the kitchen. The person escorting me opened the door to the basement, pushed me inside, and then closed it over both of us.

We stood on the top step, in the dark, as the guy held the door shut with his shoulder. I couldn't make out his face, but I suddenly realized it was the skinny, bearded guest Troy hadn't been able to place. The one he'd called just Director.

"Jesus Christ," he whispered. "Are you all right?"

"I think so," I replied.

"I guess this is what you call a melee."

Indeed, shouts and scrambling were increasing on the other side of the door. One more shot rang out. Both my new friend and I ducked.

"I didn't mean to pull you along," he said. "I just grabbed the first person I saw."

"Thanks," I said.

"I'm Johnny Cooper, by the way. I think we met at the Awards."

"Did we?"

"Yeah."

I squinted at the guy, my eyes not yet adjusted to the dark. He was using the same phony line I'd used on Alan Boilerman. Should I have been flattered? There wasn't time to decide.

"Any idea what it's all about?" he asked.

"Beats me."

"Is there a window in the basement? Can we get out?"

I thought for a second, recalling Troy's screening setup. "Yeah. But it's small, and you'll need a chair to reach it."

"Okay. That's no problem."

There was a pause, as we both stood there, breathing hard. Then, as if we were about to jump from a burning ship, he said, "Okay. Let's go."

He started down, feeling his way in the dark. But then he stopped, noticing that I wasn't following.

"What's the holdup?" he hissed. "Come on."

Through the door, I heard the disturbance, the stumbling and shouting—and one more shot. I knew that Marthe was out there. I didn't trust her, of course, but that didn't mean I could abandon her, either.

"Good luck," I said, and opened the door.

HEAD DOWN, I STARTED INTO THE FRAY, TRYING TO REACH MARTHE'S ROOM. On my way, I passed a half-opened closet. From it, two blond women peeked, afraid. I made out a third form crushed between them; it was Thor, addled as ever.

I followed a trail of olive pits, which, like bread crumbs, led me to Marthe's door.

She was coming out at the same time I was going in. She was shaking; sweat poured down her face, and she winced from what seemed a profound sciatic twinge.

"Are you all right?" I asked.

Her accent was so thick I could barely make out what she said. After a second, I realized it was: "I'm so sorry."

Then Marthe let out a gasp. When I turned to the side, I saw the guy with the gun standing in the hall, aiming his weapon. Again, it wasn't at me; he was pointing the pistol at the nearby staircase, leading up. Troy was on it, painfully taking two steps at a time.

"Don't do it!" Troy cried.

The guy didn't. He was decked by someone else, someone who flew at him and knocked him to the floor. To my shock, I recognized the bearded guy from the basement. He was a director who didn't just shout "action" but took it.

Johnny Cooper had the thug pinned. He was whomping him in the face so brutally that I had to look away. Instinctively, I pushed Marthe back into her room. She tried to pull me in but I stayed outside.

I took off after Troy instead.

Hurtling the stairs much faster than he, I caught him halfway up. Troy didn't resist. Instead, he pulled me to him. Only one big frame of his sunglasses remained intact, and his tanned face was more white than brown. He smelled as much of sweat as cologne. His voice was desperate.

"Help me, Clarence," he said.

How could I? I could give him the tape. But what if it wasn't *The Day the Clown Cried*? Either way, I wasn't handing it over.

Suddenly, on the floor above us, a door creaked opened. Troy stared up, panicked, at the room that had been the source of so much sound. He looked like a parent gazing at an endangered child.

I threw him off. Then I started up the stairs myself.

"Come back!" Troy said.

I ignored him. I was too busy gawking at the woman who had come out onto the landing. I remembered that Olivia de Haviland had replaced Joan Crawford in *Hush, Hush, Sweet Charlotte.*

There were track marks all over her arms. She looked like the hidden first wife in a junkie *Jane Eyre,* like something from the past gone bad.

It was a second before I recognized Gratey McBride. A second before I knew that she wielded an Oscar. And another before it landed on my head.

PART 4

AMSTERDAM

I WOKE UP THINKING OF ELLIOTT GOULD.

In 1971, at the height of his fame, Gould was shooting a film called *A Glimpse of Tiger,* opposite another young star of the day, Kim Darby. Then, it was alleged, his erratic behavior caused the film to be abandoned and his career to be sidetracked.

I was thinking about tigers because I was seeing visions of ocelots. Ocelots and perfume and Marthe posed beside them. Those images mixed with Gratey McBride's scary face as she hit me on the head with her award. Then I thought of flying, as I had down the stairs at Troy Kevlin's house.

The truth: I *was* flying. As I lifted my aching eyelids, I realized I was on a plane, curled up in an aisle seat like a piece of carry-on luggage. A seat belt had been loosely buckled across my middle.

"Welcome back," a voice said.

I looked over, feeling as if my head was underwater. Focusing, I recognized the man on the seat beside me. It was young, bearded Johnny Cooper, who had saved my life in Troy's house.

"Got a little headache?" he asked, pleasantly.

I tried to answer, but my mouth moved in slow-motion. No recognizable words came out.

"It must be the painkillers," he said. "I hope I didn't go overboard."

I wasn't feeling pain, that was true. I wasn't feeling anything. It was as if I was covered in a protective coating, like a little mint in a plastic wrapper. I tried to speak again, but only heard a vague, gargling sound escape my lips, and even that sounded far away.

"Can you read Marthe's letter?"

I looked where Johnny was pointing, which was into my lap. There sat a folded note written on cream-colored stationery. I opened it, saw just blurry words, none of them legible. I slowly closed it again.

"I didn't think so," he went on. "Anyway, I hope you don't mind my reading it. But it seems like you stepped into quite a hornet's nest back there. See, for years, Troy and Thor have been feeding poor Gratey McBride's drug habit, keeping her secretly in Troy's house. The mob was after Troy for money he owed them for the drugs. Marthe was trying to give her husband a new project, to get him back into the present. And you were caught in the middle."

I nodded, *very* slowly, some sense being made through my fog.

"Apparently, at a weak moment, Thor had told Howie Romaine about the sad setup with his ex. That's why Howie told Marthe that Troy might know about *The Day the Clown Cried.* See, Gratey's co-star in *Macaroon Heart,* Graus Menzies, was an extra in it, years ago." He paused. "By the way, I think Marthe really likes you."

Though incapacitated, I could still feel a sense of violation: This guy had read my private letter. Still, he'd also saved my life. Who did he think he was?

"I'm just a Hollywood guppy," he said, as if answering. "I'm not in the same league as the other guys at the party. I've only directed a couple of shorts and some videos. But the studios are starting to take an interest. I guess that's why I got on Troy's list. It was my first time at one of his parties."

I mumbled an enfeebled greeting, which sounded like "Micetoeatyou." What was Johnny Cooper doing with me?

"I want to help you," he said, as if answering, "find *The Day the Clown Cried.*"

After passing out, I woke up still on the plane. Johnny Cooper was watching the in-flight movie, headset in place.

"But where are we going?" I asked, and this time actually said the words.

Johnny didn't hear me. He was chuckling audibly at the lame black-white buddy picture. I pressed the little button for the stewardess. Soon one came over in the darkened cabin.

"Where are we going?" I asked her.

Hearing this, Johnny suddenly pulled off his headset. He gave a strained, conciliatory smile to the attendant.

"You'll have to excuse my friend," he said. "He's always kidding around."

Looking annoyed, the woman walked away. Then Johnny turned to me, still trying, with less success, to be polite.

"Look," he said, "don't call attention to yourself. We're going to Amsterdam, okay?"

Shaking his head with a swallowed "Jesus Christ," he went back to watching the film. I remembered the ferocity with which he had beaten the mobster. I thought I'd better stay on his good side. But why Amsterdam?

"That's where Graus Menzies is," he said, as if answering. "I'm a friend of a friend."

When I woke up again, I found myself in a quaint and clean little Dutch bed-and-breakfast. My room looked out on an immaculate garden. My packed bags sat in a corner. I had no memory of getting there. I assumed the solicitous Johnny Cooper had carried me in his arms.

I assumed I was there on his dime, too. So the first thing I did was phone Dena at her dad's in Maine.

"I've been worried sick," she said. "When I called L.A., a guy with a gravelly voice told me just 'the Angel has flown.' Then he hung up."

"That was Troy," I told her. "I'm surprised he's still alive."

"After that, I tried your mother in New Jersey. A woman there told me that because of lack of money, your mother 'just had a relapse.' Did I do something wrong?"

I sighed, deeply, thinking of Aunt Ruby. "No. Not at all."

I explained my strange arrival in Amsterdam, making sure to add that clues might be forthcoming, from an actual cast member of *Clown*.

"But have you watched the tape?" she asked.

My head still thick, I remembered its existence. Did I tell Johnny Cooper about it? Probably not; I'd been unable to say much of anything.

"I, uh, don't think so," I said.

There was a long pause, as Dena clearly reevaluated my efficiency. She took on her familiar, quiet, somewhat irritated tone. "I'm not going to ask what happened in L.A., Roy. But I found diaries of my father's. They've had a lot of water damage, but you can still read some of them. Maybe there's something there. I'm going to copy and fax the remaining pages to you. Do you think you'll be able to handle it?"

I tried to restrain some knee-jerk pique. Still, Dena had a point. I had gotten nothing from Howie Romaine and nearly been killed at Troy Kevlin's. Second-case jitters, I told myself; the sophomore jinx, as they say in showbiz.

Dena, however, was still completely competent, undeterred even by sentiment in her dead father's house. I thought of *The Only Game in Town,* the 1970 movie in which Warren Beatty had replaced Frank Sinatra opposite Elizabeth Taylor. The result was a mismatch. I didn't share this info with her.

"Of course I can handle it," I said, my voice unfortunately cracking. I rustled up hotel stationery with the address. Then I told her where to fax the pages.

"Well, look on the bright side," she said. "The guy chasing you probably won't come overseas."

"That's true," I said, considering it.

"Take care of yourself, Roy," she said, with sudden, reluctant affection.

"You, too," I said, with a similar sound, and hung up.

I looked to see if Johnny had packed my laptop. He had. Then I checked my e-mail.

Dear Milano,

Before you read it in the trades, here's a news flash: I've quit Quelman. *The love story was just the beginning of how the suits wanted to screw up the franchise. I simply couldn't live with myself and continue.*

Needless to say, now that I'm off the project, we'll have to declare my financial support in our Clown *agreement null and void. (Please refer to clause three in our deal memo, referring to "unforeseen circumstances.") But good luck with it.*

Abner

P.S. Don't contact me at the Riverside Drive number. Taylor and I have gone our separate ways. New phone/mail info TK.

If my brain was cloudy before, it swiftly cleared up. Lying through his teeth about the cause, Abner had left me penniless in a European city, where I had been—convivially, I admit—kidnapped. I had nothing to send my mother and no way to get home. I was completely at the mercy of Johnny Cooper. Childishly, I swore that, if I had anything to say about it, Abner would never, ever see *The Day the Clown Cried.*

It didn't matter what I thought. I immediately opened my bags and rifled through them.

The tape was gone.

I HAD NO TIME TO COME UP WITH A CAUSE. THERE WAS KNOCKING AT THE door.

"Like the place?" Johnny asked, in his pleasant way. "I'm on the floor above. Graus is, too."

"It's fine," I said, discombobulated.

"You're looking perkier. That sleep must have done you good."

"Thanks. It must have been quite a, uh, dose you gave me."

"Well, you got quite a bump on the bean."

I hadn't even thought of that. I moved over to a tastefully ornate mirror. A welt the size of a kumquat decorated the left side of my head.

"Jesus," I said.

"People say what Oscars can do for your career, but they never mention what they can do to your head."

Johnny laughed, and so did I. He was a disarming guy, despite his occasionally vicious temper. I couldn't help it; I felt grateful to him, regardless of his motive. I wondered, though: What *was* his motive?

"I really hope we can find the movie," he said, as if answering. "I know there's no point in contacting Jerry. I'm a big buff in general. Maybe one day I'll make a film somebody cares to see as much as they do *Clown*. That's my dream."

I waited to reply. Then his seeming lack of guile opened me up. "Another famous uncompleted film is Josef von Sternberg's adaptation of Robert Graves's *I, Claudius,* from the thirties. Charles Laughton and Merle Oberon were in it."

"Sure," he said. "I've seen the documentary about it. What was shot looked phenomenal. It's a real shame."

"Right," I said, surprised he knew. "The documentary."

"Do you know about *Lazy River,* from the thirties, too? Tod Browning was directing it. Erskine Caldwell and William Faulkner were writing it. Jean Harlow and Lionel Barrymore were starring. That was also abandoned. Imagine seeing that one!"

I felt faint again, but not from being smashed on the head. This time, I'd been hit by a realization. I'd never heard of that movie.

Was it possible that Johnny Cooper knew more about movies than I did? As a functional filmmaker, he really couldn't be considered trivial. His beard even grew in pretty well. Shouldn't I hate this guy?

"What about *Soldier Lad*?" I asked. "With Wallace Beery and Helen Hayes? That was probably another uncompleted masterpiece."

Johnny just looked at me, blankly. "You got me on that one. Never heard of it."

I felt lousy then. I'd made it up. Quickly, I changed the subject.

"Did anyone go through my bag, do you know?" I asked.

"Your bag? Not that I know of. Why? Is something missing?"

"No. No. It's all right."

Protectively, I zipped up my luggage. Maybe I'd left the tape in California.

"Come on," Johnny said. "Graus is waiting."

Graus Menzies *was* waiting, next door. He was sitting in the shadows of an Amsterdam coffeehouse, or legal marijuana den. The place was a dump, virtually unfurnished, with only a few old wooden chairs and tables. Apparently, the pot was enough; nothing else was needed.

If Graus was impatient for our appearance, you'd never have known it. He was busy pontificating to a small, attractive redhead of thirty, while sucking deeply on a joint.

Like most movie actors, he was tiny with a big handsome head. About sixty, he had lots of salt-and-pepper hair and a face with outsized features—buggy eyes, a sharp nose, a harshly cut mouth. A scarf was twirled stylishly around his neck.

After starring in acclaimed German films in the Seventies, Graus had made an American splash with *Macaroon Heart*. Now he had been reduced to playing supporting Nazis in Hollywood potboilers. The declension had taken its toll: He had a reputation for bad behavior, womanizing, and drinking. Like Howie Romaine and Troy Kevlin, he, too, had written a memoir—*I Am Graus!*—but it was considered libelous, quickly pulled from U.S. stores, and reedited. The full, uncensored edition was a sought-after collector's item. Or so my book trivia friends told me.

"Graus," Johnny said, amiably, sitting down. "Here's the guy I wanted you to meet."

"Hold on, little boy!" Graus yelled at him. Then he finished the story he was telling the girl. The punch line was "I am Graus!" and he barked it like a dog.

The girl, an American, laughed, appreciatively. She, too, seemed stoned, and it made her squint appealingly. She had short red hair, freckles, and bright blue eyes, which she now directed, with sweet fuzziness, at me.

"This is Katie Emond," Johnny said. "She was the publicist on Graus's book in the States. Now she's his assistant."

"My assistant—of love!" Graus yelled. He started to chew comically on the girl's bare upper arm, while crying, "I am Graus!"

Katie, who was shaking my hand at the time, giggled wildly. Then Johnny slipped onto the chair beside her, kissed her cheek, and draped his arm familiarly around her shoulder. She kissed him, too, on the neck. He was clearly a very good friend of a friend.

"Graus," Johnny said. "This is Roy Milano. He's the fan I told you about."

Johnny had warned me to be vague and polite in my questions. Apparently, Katie, ever protective of Graus, should be handled with care, as well.

Graus's stare became somewhat hooded as he checked me out. "Right. Right. My 'fan.' " He extended the end of a wet, collapsing joint to me. I waved it away, but his offer stayed good. When I muttered a courteous "No, thank you," he brought down the drug very slowly, with an expression of disgust. Then he immediately switched his attention to Johnny and Katie.

"Did I ever tell you two about the chambermaid I shtupped in 1974?"

The younger people rolled their eyes and smiled, indulgently.

"She was an Austrian," he went on. "Beautiful. Pigtails, like Heidi. Every morning, she made my bed, and I would play rumpy-pumpy with her. I was always late to the set. I'm lucky I was working for Wim Wenders, otherwise curtains for Graus the louse."

"That was in Chapter Eight of your book," Katie said, giggling again. "Except I think you said she was Swiss."

Graus made kissing sounds at her. "In the uncensored version. You know everything, little girl. That's why I love you." Then he turned, suddenly and coldly, to me. "That's all I remember about my life, that chambermaid. You want to know any more?"

"Well," I said, stupidly answering, "actually, yes, I'd very much like to know about *The Day*—"

"Forget it, Charlie! That's the end of the line, last stop, everyone out! I got no more to say!"

Graus buried his face in a mug of beer, which sat, half-finished, on the table. I sensed tension in his companions now. When he finished drinking, Graus slowly licked the foam from his mouth, and looked right at Katie and Johnny.

"Tell your scummy friend to leave or I'll kill him," he said.

I assumed this was an exaggeration, like everything else he had said.

A second later, I learned it wasn't.

GRAUS SPRANG AT ME LIKE A SMALL OLD LION.

The two of us went flying onto the dirty floor. Growling and barking, smelling of dope and beer, he pummeled me, as we rolled around. I tried pushing him away, but he held me in a hug, one surprisingly hard to break.

"I'll kill you before I tell you anything," he whispered in my ear.

I brought my knee up into his groin, but he didn't recoil. To my shock, Graus seemed gratified by the impact, and he groaned with what appeared pleasure.

"Little tiger," he said. Then he made to sink his teeth into my ear.

Luckily, he never got a chance. A second later, he was choking.

"Gaaak," Graus gurgled.

The silk scarf around his neck had been tightened. He coughed again with an expression of surprise. Then his eyes, which already protruded, grew even bigger.

I looked up. Johnny stood there, holding the end of the scarf in a tight grip, yanking on it as if it were the reins of a feisty horse. Then, with what seemed superhuman strength, he pulled Graus's compact body up and off of me.

Still using the scarf as a lead, he jerked the older man to him. When they stood nose to nose, he jammed a hand into his own pants pocket. He came out with a little paring knife, which gleamed in the bar's dim light. Graus's eyes grew impossibly large and his "gaaak"ing became more alarmed and birdlike.

Johnny waved the weapon in front of the actor's eyes. Then, with one swift snap, he cut the scarf, freeing Graus. The movement was so sudden that the sybarite stumbled back, and plopped directly onto a chair.

My savior wasn't finished with him. He quickly approached the seated Graus, who seemed genuinely dazed. Drawing his right hand back, swiftly, Johnny slapped him in the face. The cracking sound echoed through the nearly empty place. Raising his mitt once more, Johnny backhanded him.

He was not about to stop. He made to strike again. There was something parental and sadistic about the beating. It seemed like child abuse, though Graus predated us all.

"That's enough!" Katie yelled.

Johnny's hand stopped in mid-threat. He glanced at his girlfriend, whose eyes pleaded with him, though vaguely. Then he looked at his victim, whose cheeks were beet red and whose lips emitted a tiny speck of blood. There was a pause before a decision was made.

"One more," Graus whispered.

Johnny nodded. It was the hardest blow of all, and the actor's head flipped back like a ricochet. Then it came forward and his chin settled on his chest, his wild hair hung in his eyes, and a trickle of blood discolored his chin.

There was silence for a second. Then, panting, Johnny looked down at the floor, where I was still lying.

"You okay, pal?" he asked me, with his usual concern.

I didn't know what to say. I was relatively unhurt. But okay?

Johnny didn't wait for me to answer. He held out a friendly hand—the palm red from beating Graus Menzies—and pulled me up.

"Sorry Graus couldn't be more helpful," he said. "I think he'll open up when he knows you better."

"Oh," I said, shaken. "Okay. But will he be—"

"He'll be fine," Katie said, pleasant again. "This is just, you know, a thing we do."

"Now go get washed up for dinner. You ever have 'ricetable'? It's a Dutch specialty."

Katie was nodding, vigorously. "It's delicious!" she agreed.

"Tastes good," Graus even said, though very quietly.

His assistant rose from her doobis haze and administered to Graus. With a table napkin, Katie wiped off his face and then carefully recombed his hair. The older man found the strength to place his hands on her behind and squeeze.

Somewhat stunned, I sat and stared. But then the look on Johnny's face became threatening again, after having shifted to gentleness. That made me move.

"Hey, I like your friend," I heard Katie say, sincerely, as I left.

I headed back to my room, determined to flee Amsterdam. After Howie, Troy, Marthe, Thor, and Gratey, here was yet another curdled piece of the past, and one more weirdo family. How much did Graus know about *Clown*, anyway? Was it worth putting up with *this*? If I could only find the tape, I might not need anyone's help, I could get the hell out.

I hesitated, recalling Johnny's weird, mercurial personality. He had rescued me—twice, now. He seemed sincere about helping. At the same time, he was fast with fists and knives and willing to engage in erotic pain games with an iconic has-been. I also thought of Katie's pretty face; she had said she liked me. Mixed feelings and motives slowed my resolve.

Then something stopped it entirely. Dena's fax had arrived: excerpts from her father's diary.

ALL FORTY-EIGHT PAGES OF THEM.

The elderly lady who owned the B&B, who had been so polite when I met her, now looked at me with disgust. Carrying the piles of paper that had jammed her machine, I went, mortified, to my room.

I laid the pages on my bed, as if they were pieces of a puzzle. Then, completely wiped out, I fell asleep beside them.

In the morning, I began to read.

The surviving entries in Ted Savitch's diary scanned the last forty or so years of the twentieth century, though commented only briefly on most of it. There were passages ranging from two words in 1977 (*Head cold!*) to a longer discourse on money problems in 1990 (*No light, all tunnel.*).

The day of his wedding in 1968 inspired just two lines: *Mistake of lifetime? Fingers crossed!* Touchingly, a rapturous entry concerned the birth of his daughter, Dena, in 1974.

> What little hands, what little feet! . . . You can see the whole future in her face . . . Whole question of support—money—looms, however . . .

The ensuing disintegration of his family life was painful. Two years later, there was a description of how he had separated, then returned, to his wife:

> Trying to make a go . . . Not easy . . . Little Dena a heartbreaker . . . Sometimes think only happy time alone in movie theater . . . Guilt at thinking that, but true.

Movies were a frequent subject, and, as he mentioned, a rare occasion for happiness. His wife, it turned out, had no interest in them: *Why must she make fun of it?* He provided lots of capsule reviews that aped professional criticism: *Godfather Two—Two long! . . . Peter Sellers is back as Clouseau and more clueless than ever!*

There was also a long, impassioned account of an adulterous one-night stand in 1969 that started in a movie theater. Ted had attended a double feature at one of the now long-gone grind houses on Forty-second Street in Manhattan. The bill consisted of *One More Time,* a sequel reuniting the stars of 1968's comedy *Salt and Pepper,* Sammy Davis Jr. and Peter Lawford. It was the only film Jerry Lewis directed in which he didn't appear. The other picture was *Ace High,* a spaghetti western with Eli Wallach. The movies may have been minor, but the affair was Oscar-worthy:

> She was in town from the suburbs . . . Married, like me . . . Sat next to me . . . Would I scare her off if I said something, I wondered? . . . Sammy Davis and Peter Lawford were mugging onscreen . . . "It's no *Salt and Pepper,*" she whispered to me, suddenly, and she was right . . . Before the second feature, I kissed her . . . The hotel was only blocks away . . . We talked about movies before and after sex . . . It was incredible . . . We knew each other's names, but that was all . . .

He had clearly found a kindred spirit. He seemed to follow up on the encounter, futilely. One entry recounts his wife asking about long-distance charges in the phone bill: *How many times did I call and hang up? Pathetic, and now had to lie about it.* Then the whole thing was lost to the past.

By 1980, he had left his family for good and lived alone. He didn't write about secretly photographing Dena as she grew up. But he was clearly most comfortable just seeing her on film: *My own wonderful little movie . . .*

The rest of the diary no longer existed.

I finished what I'd read with a feeling of empathy. Dena's father had been unrequited, and had committed to a family he didn't want and couldn't support. It was too bad he hadn't lived later, when trivial people could find a community, instead of sneaking around like perverts. After all, I felt that's what Ted Savitch had been, in the deepest sense of the word: trivial.

I forced myself to snap back to the matter at hand. There had been no mention of *The Day the Clown Cried.* Could such a dreamer ever have gotten his hands on such a score? If I didn't find the tape again, I might never know.

I tried to be discreet when I called Dena. I had noticed a splotch on the last diary page, which was probably food but might have been tears.

"Pretty interesting," I said. "But it doesn't really get us anywhere."

"Thanks for the review," she said, with surprising testiness. "It *is* a man's life, you know." Then she got in a dig. "How about the tape?"

I tried to sound secure. "Any minute now." The excruciating moment passed. "How long will you be in Bar Harbor?"

"Until the end of the week. If I don't learn anything else."

"And then?"

"Don't know."

This quest had clearly given Dena's life some structure; maybe that had been the point of it, after all. When it ended, where would she be? I knew the feeling.

"You?" she said.

Luckily, before I could answer, a knock came at the door. Resting the receiver on my shoulder, I opened it.

Katie the assistant was standing there. She wore shorts and a T-shirt that hiked appealingly above her stomach. Her hair was the color of fire. She pantomimed a bike ride invitation in a way that made me laugh.

"Roy?" Dena said, in my ear.

"What?"

"What's so funny?"

"Nothing. What do you mean?"

"Look," Dena said, "what are you actually *doing* there in Amsterdam?"

I gestured to Katie that I'd be off in a minute. She gave me a thumbs-up, and a cute little muscle flexed in her bare arm.

"I think," I said, "that I'm about to learn something."

ONE BIKE WITH TWO SEATS AND FOUR PEDALS WAS PARKED OUTSIDE. I hadn't ridden since high school and hadn't even seen a tandem since childhood. But Katie scoffed at my hesitation.

"How fast can we go?" she said, getting on the front seat. "Besides, everybody rides in Amsterdam."

It was true. As we pumped along the cobblestone "Straats," "Pleins," and "Grachts," as we took small bridges above canals, it seemed like we had joined an army of cyclists. I only fell off twice, and Katie was nice enough not to laugh. Too loudly.

She laughed about virtually everything. Apparently, the grind of New York publishing—and normal employment in general—hadn't agreed with her. Katie had babysat the louche and dissolute Graus through a disastrous book tour. Then she accepted his bleary offer to come work for him.

"If you can call it work," she said. "Either way, it's better than nine to five. That wasn't for me."

I was no match for the athletic Katie, who stood up, attractively, to push up and down on her pedals.

"Well, it's definitely not boring!" I called, panting.

She laughed again, looking back. "It's lucky I'm open to new experiences! Sorry about the one yesterday, though!"

"You mean—" How could I put it decorously? "Beating up Graus in the pot bar?"

"Right!" Laughing. "We had to improv that one pretty fast! See, we re-create exciting scenes from old movies! It was Johnny's idea, once he found out what Graus was, you know, into! Johnny's been teaching me a lot about them, movies. The best he could come up with yesterday was *Frenzy,* the Hitchcock picture! Did you ever see it?"

"Of course! The necktie killer!"

"Right! We had to use Graus's scarf! Not the same thing!"

This was of great prurient interest. I dragged a foot on the ground, unsubtlely. We rested on a bridge.

"How did you meet Johnny?" I asked.

"At a party in New York. He got a kick that I work for Graus. Right now, we're in town shooting a new movie. Graus plays a Nazi. *Again.*"

The typecasting was a shift from how he'd started his career: as a concentration camp inmate. Now seemed like a good time for a segue. "It must bring him back to his days as an extra."

"Probably," she said, shrugging.

I jumped in, ignoring Johnny's directive. "What do you know about *The Day the Clown Cried*?"

"What do I know about it? Or what do I know about what Graus knows about it?" From someone else, it might have sounded hostile. Yet Katie retained a weird sunniness, even while stonewalling. She clearly wanted to experience and express every emotion, just to see how it felt.

"About what Graus knows."

She shrugged again. "I don't know much." The answer seemed guarded. Then I realized it was just indifference.

Katie now leaned onto my shoulder to adjust her sneaker. Her hand staying and resting there, she asked me, "Why do you want to know so much, anyway, Roy?"

"What do you mean?"

"Why not just enjoy what you can't know? Leave things open? That's how I like it."

No wonder Graus dug Katie. Besides her obvious physical appeal, she was a throwback to the actor's sexy, searching, seventies heyday. But trivial people, not to mention detectives, need certainty.

"I wish I could," I said, somewhat insincerely. "But I can't."

As I feared it might, this made her remove her hand. "You're a man on a mission?"

"You could put it that way."

"Well," she scrunched up her face, with imitation seriousness, "be careful."

Was she kidding? "What do you mean? Why?"

Katie turned her head, then pointed it. "Because that guy over there's been watching us."

"What guy?"

I looked where she pointed. Another cyclist stood across the canal, leaning against a building. He wore a bike rider's spandex outfit; a skull-cap and goggles completed the ensemble.

"There have been a lot of robberies around here lately," she said. "Maybe we ought to get going."

I was surprised at such trepidation from carefree Katie. The street couldn't have looked more placid and residential. Or, come to think of it, more empty, now that the workday had begun. Maybe she had a point.

"Get on," she said, "and let's go."

Katie didn't wait; she straddled the lead position as decisively as a Hell's Angel would his hog. I got on the back, trying to keep up. Then we took off.

The other guy did, too.

"Is he coming?" Katie asked.

"Yes!"

"Damn!"

The three of us rode on parallel sides of the street, separated by water. Occasionally, we passed another tiny bridge, which linked the two parts of the *gracht*. For now, the guy was safely behind.

"Catching up?"

"Not so far!"

"Good!"

We passed over another bridge. When I turned to look across, I didn't see him anymore.

"I think we lost him!" I called.

"What?"

"I said I think we—"

I turned to look again, virtually turned my head around. The bicyclist had taken the bridge, and was now on our side. And gaining.

"Forget what I said!"

"What?"

"He's coming closer!"

"Okay then! Hold on!"

"What?"

"I said, hold on!"

KATIE STOOD IN THE SADDLE AGAIN.

I was too rattled to ogle her. My heart rose as she did, and I could feel the blood in my ears.

We zoomed past rows and rows of adorable, identical Dutch brownstones. Soon all I saw were blurred colors; the city became an Impressionist painting, courtesy of Katie. I had no choice but to dig in, and my tortured legs hammered up and down.

I hoped Katie knew what she was doing. I thought that Jack Nicholson had replaced Rip Torn in *Easy Rider* and Lee Marvin had replaced Keenan Wynn in *The Wild One.*

When I turned, the guy was even closer.

My head bobbing, I couldn't focus on his face; but beneath the goggles, he seemed to be grinning, crazily.

I turned forward again. The neighborhood was coming to an end. Too soon, the street would gutter out into a commercial block catering to tourists. I saw a big, corny windmill above a tacky restaurant.

There was one last bridge over a last canal before we got there. My mind racing as fast as the bike, I thought that Alec Guinness had replaced Charles Laughton in *The Bridge on the River Kwai.* Laughton was too fat to be bought as a prisoner of war.

The whiz of wheels was now right behind my head.

I flared around, unable to resist seeing our pursuer. He had the same strange gritted-teeth look, only more extreme, the effort of the chase taking its toll. But he wasn't too tired to do something new.

He reached out to grab our bike.

His fingers clawed at the rat-trap above our back rear tire. He fell away. Then he tried again. Katie and I managed to pedal fast enough to keep him ever reaching, never taking hold. But how long could we keep on doing it?

"Don't stop!" I yelled, more at myself than her.

"Don't worry!" Katie responded.

Once more, the guy flung out his hand. This time, his fingers tapped the steel of the rat-trap. Either he was getting better or we were getting worse.

The final bridge was just a few feet away. I thought I could even hear tinny, piped-in music from the windmill restaurant.

I turned around again and saw him. I noticed another detail on what was left bare of his face. There were shaving cuts on his chin and cheeks. I took a second to consider it. That was a mistake.

He got hold of the back of the bike.

Brutally now, as he rode, he began waving our bike back and forth on the cobblestone road. I felt myself veering, nearly tipping over. Katie kept more of a steady hand, but even she had to hold on tight. The bridge was steps away, and water, of course, was underneath it.

"Hey!" I yelled to him, absurdly.

He gave us a particularly hard yank to the right. My upper half tilted over as if directly pushed. It took all my strength to lean left, sit back firmly on the seat, while pedaling with all my might.

Now we were on the bridge. Beyond it was the street of shops and eats, home of help or even worse hurt. I saw the spokes of the windmill start to move, ever so slowly.

Then I realized it wasn't moving. I was.

The guy had given the tandem a final, galvanizing pull to the side. The back tire skidded once, definitively, and my hands lost their grip. I sailed from my seat.

For a second, I saw only Amsterdam sky. Then, on my way down, I saw a little boat, a *skip* I think they call it, docked in the canal. A cat sat on its protective tarp. It calmly watched me hit the water.

IT WAS ONLY DEEP ENOUGH TO DROWN ME.

I headed to the bottom, dark water filling my nose and mouth. I smelled unwashed feet and, strangely, almonds. I thought that Katharine Hepburn had fallen into a Venetian canal in David Lean's *Summertime,* and the result was a lifelong eye infection.

In the eighties, an elderly Lean was announced to direct a film of Joseph Conrad's *Nostromo* starring Dennis Quaid. He died before it happened; on deck was Arthur Penn, who'd been hired as an insurance hedge. But the film was scuttled, anyway. A few years earlier, Penn had been replaced on *Altered States* by Ken Russell.

Underwater, these thoughts swam around my brain like the little fish darting around my head. Or were they just pieces of dirt? I couldn't tell, and opening my eyes only caused stinging. I squeezed them shut again. Then I tried to rise.

I felt a ten-ton weight on my head.

It took me a second to realize that it was a hand, pressing upon my skull. Sitting on the bottom now, I reached up and, with ten fingers, grabbed ahold of what felt like a male forearm. When frantic jerking of the arm solved nothing, I sank my nails into its skin.

It took a surprisingly long time for the arm's pressure to subside. When, at last, it succumbed, it wasn't to my stabbing; I faintly heard a woman's voice.

"That's enough!" it said.

Then the hand pushed me over, in a last aggressive act.

I fell in slow motion, my chest scorched from lack of air. Just before hitting the filthy canal floor, I managed to right myself in time to survive. I shot to the surface and emerged, spitting and moaning, like an angry whale.

Standing there—it really was shallow—I looked around at the streets and bridges. I saw no one, not the bicyclist, not Katie. I didn't think about a motive or the identity of the perpetrator. I was too stunned.

Then, a second later, I was too confused.

Feet away, Katie and the spandex man were standing, leaning on their bikes, outside the windmill restaurant. They were talking, casually. Wiping dirty water from my eyes, I saw that the guy had removed his hat and goggles.

It was Johnny Cooper, newly shaven. Katie was kissing him.

The two of them turned. They saw me standing there, helplessly, in the canal. Then they both waved at me, and smiled.

"What do you mean, it was *The Postman Always Rings Twice*?" I shouted.

"We were doing a scene from it," Katie explained. "Unfortunately, neither one of us owns a car. So we did the best we could. Graus is busy working."

The three of us were having lunch in the tacky tourist trap, appropriately named The Wooden Shoes. My soaked and stinky appearance caused little gawking from other tables; the Dutch are, of course, discreet.

"The scene in the car where Lana Turner and John Garfield kill her husband?" Johnny said. "That's what we were doing. Only on bikes."

There was a long pause, as I tried to take in both the information and the undercooked onion soup. Re-creating the scene meant I had been

Cecil Kellaway, the pudgy, middle-aged character actor who played Lana Turner's cuckold. I didn't know whether to be offended, furious, or afraid. I felt a little bit of each.

I directed my attention to Johnny's tight, black, rolled-up sleeve. His forearm held the scars of my defensive attack. There could be no doubt I'd heard them right.

"Look," I said, suddenly famished, chewing on stale bread, "I don't know what Graus likes. But I—"

"We considered doing *From Here to Eternity,*" Johnny said, pleasantly. "The love scene on the beach? Deborah Kerr, Burt Lancaster—and Philip Ober was the husband she cheated on."

"There's no murder in that," Katie scoffed.

"That's what I'm *saying,*" Johnny told her. "It would have been too much of an embellishment. So instead it was *Postman.*"

"Not the remake." Katie giggled.

"That's right," he agreed. "We kept our clothes on."

"Though it might have been *Don't Look Now.* With the canals and all, in Venice? The last scene, with the—" Katie mimed a vicious stabbing.

"True, that's true. That would have made me Donald Sutherland. And you the mad dwarf."

"Julie Christie," Katie shook her head.

"Mad dwarf," Johnny shot back.

"You."

"You."

I found myself breaking in. "Did you know that Ian Holm replaced Donald Sutherland in *The Sweet Hereafter*?"

There was a pause, as each turned to me, slowly, from their flirting. Johnny smiled, politely.

"Yes," he said. "I knew that."

I said nothing else then. The meaning of the last film's title—its intimations of the afterworld—unsettled me. The two had tried to kill me. Or, more specifically, Johnny had. Or was it all in fun?

Either way, it seemed a high price to pay for information about *The Day the Clown Cried.* If Graus had any, to begin with.

"Come on," Johnny said, as if this were indeed my payment. "Let's get you cleaned up and go see Graus." He rubbed his clean chin. "Hey, how do you like my new look?"

Graus Menzies was running the SS. He stood in the center of the city's huge flower market, surrounded by camera equipment, technicians, and other actors. Dressed in a Nazi uniform, he took a sniper's gunshot to the chest, which exploded a squib hidden on him.

It was a movie called *Beach Head,* in which Nazis time-travel to the present and fight spring-break students. The actor was playing fifth banana to Wally Caking, a rubber-faced comic refugee from MTV.

Graus was having trouble with the timing of his scream, turn, and fall. Apparently, it wasn't the first time that day.

"Cut!" an exasperated voice cried.

A young, moussed director flew out of a chair and started screaming at him in English. The actor, who was lying on the ground, took a while to find his feet. After he did, he painstakingly brushed himself off. The director continued to berate him. Graus waited for the guy to finish. Then he spat in his face.

"Uh-oh," Johnny said, from our vantage point a few feet away.

The two began a vein-popping shriekfest, punctuated by American and German curses. It took four crew members to separate them. As Graus was led away, he yelled, "For Fassbinder, maybe! But not for you!"

Lunch was called. After being painfully stripped of his squib, Graus joined us, his chest heaving, sweat dripping from his face.

"When that video pig gets to hell, he'll find me there," Graus said.

"Chill out, Graus," Katie said, agreeably.

Hearing that, I thought the actor would literally explode. Instead, disarmed, murmuring "Little boy and little girl," he kissed and hugged Katie and Johnny. He was about to do the same to me, when he caught himself.

"Ucch," he shuddered, and turned away.

Perhaps this wasn't the best time to grill him on his past. "I'll kill you before I tell you anything," he had said, when he tried to eat me in the bar. Had that been anything but hyperbole? I would have been happy to find out later.

"When you get a minute, Roy here still wants to chat with you," Johnny said, heedlessly. "It's about *The Day the Clown Cried*."

Graus looked at me. His heavily made-up face was the color of a polluted sunset. Fake bloodstains soaked the shirt beneath his uniform.

"Do you want more of what I just gave that director?" he shouted. "I told you I don't want to talk! Store closed! Out of business!"

"Well, actually," I said, uneasily, "you suggested that you would just rather see me dead before you—"

"Sorry! I can't hear you! I've gone deaf!" Graus started doing a crazy parody of sign language.

Soon Johnny and Katie were following his lead, their fingers flying, "answering" him, laughing like kids. Graus drew them into one more group hug.

I began to slowly back away. I was getting fed up with their mood swings. Also, I liked information more, and yelling and physical pain less, than they.

The filming started again. I figured that that would buy me some time. I saw only Katie turn and casually notice I was gone.

The time for fooling around was over. I headed quickly back to the B&B. If Graus had anything to tell me, I might find it in his room.

SNEAKING INTO SOMEONE'S PLACE WAS MORE FOR THIEVES THAN DETECTIVES. But desperate times called for desperate measures.

I waited until the chambermaid started doing her rounds.

Graus's door was left open, after the woman, barely more than a teenager, entered. I walked soundlessly on flowered carpet until I reached the threshold. Peeking in, I soon saw that she had entered the bathroom, and that her back was to me.

I slipped inside.

Recognizing that the room was identical to my own—bed, table, TV/VCR, not much else—I knew just where the closet was. So it didn't take me long to open and then close its door over me.

Graus's clothes smelled of all kinds of smoke.

It was almost dusk, and fading light streamed in through the slats in the door. Standing straight in the compressed space, I could only bend my head slightly and I couldn't move my arms at all. I hoped the maid would be finished soon.

Then someone else entered the room.

Graus was already home. I shouldn't have been surprised; his behavior had suggested he wouldn't be long for the set. But my heart pounded deafeningly as he shut, then locked, the room's door.

He greeted the maid by her first name.

She gave a startled little cry, then a muffled laugh. I stared through the skinny openings in the closet door. It was hard for the girl to be heard with her mouth buried in Graus's neck.

The actor used to like chambermaids, and, apparently, his taste hadn't changed. I saw glimpses of the two grappling, the girl yipping, Graus growling. Then they moved to the—out of sight—bed.

Starting to sweat a little, I thought that Gene Hackman had replaced George Segal who replaced Michael Moriarty in *Lucky Lady*.

The sounds of brutal sex play continued, grew in volume and intensity—slaps, bites, and "I am Graus!"—until they subsided.

Then the complaining began.

Even though he spoke in German, I could tell Graus was bitching about the day's work. The phrases *Fassbinder* and *video pig* were unmistakable. The girl whispered to calm him down, then did something else in silence, and it seemed to work. In a second, his comments were quiet, grateful, and almost inaudible.

Then I heard him rise.

Through the closet, I now saw terrifying glimpses of a naked Graus Menzies. His bulging eyes, barrel gut, and hairy back rocking my world, he came right toward me. Then he started to open the closet.

I backed up through Graus's aromatic wardrobe, flattening myself against the closet wall, hidden by slacks, shirts, and ties. Crouching, the actor reached a stubby hand in and grabbed a bag up off the floor. Then he pulled back, without seeing me, and shut the door again.

I stepped forward and groped my way out of the silk and wool curtain. I pressed my face right up against the closet slats. Simian in his nudity, Graus now took a videotape from the bag, shook it from its box, and stuck it into the VCR. Then he moved out of view, back to the bed, to watch with his friend.

The TV faced away from the closet; I couldn't see the screen. So I directed my ear to a slat, trying to hear any sound from what I assumed was a porno flick.

I heard nothing. Then, after a while, there came a voice.

It was Graus's. He was mumbling. Then he was screaming, incredulously, in perfectly audible English.

"*Home movies?*" he said. "*Home movies!*"

Furiously, he approached the TV. Nearly punching the machine, he popped the tape out. Then he jammed it, cursing a blue streak, back into its box.

I recognized the tape as mine. Or, more precisely, as Dena's father's.

There was frenzied dressing, as Graus barked at his playmate to hurry. Holding his shoes and socks—and the tape—Graus fled the room, followed by the maid, clutching her clothing closed. After a second, the room door shut.

I waited, fearing their return. Then, after a proper interval, I ran from the place myself.

On the top step of the stairs that led to my own hall, I stopped again. Graus was banging on my door.

"Come out, little scum boy!" he was saying. "I know what you did!" Then he added, with mockery, "Don't worry! I won't hurt you!"

Finally, disgusted, fuming, he walked away.

Cautiously, I sneaked in.

I raced around my room, not sure what I meant to do. Instinctively, and irrationally, I started to pack, prepared again to flee.

The tape *had* been stolen. It wasn't *Clown;* it was, most probably, footage Dena's father took of her as a child. Graus had been surprised to see it, so he wasn't a suspect. He thought I had replaced his porn with it. But why would I have done that?

I was pretty sure I knew who had.

As I stuffed my clothes into my bags, a piece of paper fluttered out. I stooped to retrieve it. I recognized it as Marthe's letter, folded in its cream stationery.

It had only been read to me by Johnny on the plane; I'd never perused it myself. So, hastily, I unfolded and scanned it.

Most of the information was familiar: Gratey, Thor, Troy. Regret about *Clown*. Then a few lines at the end told me something new.

> I don't know who this Johnny Cooper is. He wasn't invited to Troy's party. He was crashing in. *(sic)* No one ever heard of him. Just a head up *(sic)*

I glanced up from the page, feeling chilled. Suddenly, a merry knock came at the door. Shave and a haircut, two bits.

"Come on!" Johnny called. "Let's have some fun!"

WE WERE GOING TO HAARLEM.

Not Harlem, Haarlem. It was a town north of Amsterdam, known for its cosmopolitan center and famous art museum. A train ride would show me the Dutch countryside at dusk. . . . At least that's what Johnny and Katie told me.

The compartment was first class; we had it to ourselves. It was palatial and elegant, nothing like a dingy American commuter train. Yet enjoying the exotic aspects of another country was the last thing on my mind. Sitting opposite them, I couldn't stop staring at Johnny.

"I wish Graus could have come," he said benignly. "But they called him back to the set for some pickups."

"He seemed to have been loaded for bear," Katie said. "Pissed off about something."

"Is that right?" Johnny asked. "Huh."

"Yeah, I wonder why that is," I said, pointedly, never taking my eyes off him.

He didn't take the bait, only pointed out the window.

"Look at the fields, Roy," he said. "You can actually see tulips."

"Fascinating," I said.

There was an uncomfortable silence. Katie kept looking confusedly at the two of us. Something told me that, no matter what was happening, she was innocent of it. At least I hoped so.

"How about a little—" Johnny gestured between the cars and made the universal symbol for dope smoking.

"None for me, thanks," Katie said, curling up for a nap.

"Roy?"

I shook my head no. But, yawning, Katie gave me a scowly face.

"Go on," she said. "It might cheer you up. Everyone's so grumpy today."

In a second she was asleep. Johnny kept staring at me, the only sound the mild hum of the modern train. Maybe being alone with him was the answer now, I thought. The prospect, however, made me shaky.

"Okay," I said.

We stood in the narrow space between cars, sheltered from the ground on either side by chains. If I strained, I could see passengers through the glass doors before and behind us. Otherwise, it was just me, Johnny, and the quickly darkening world.

He lit up the joint, took a deep toke. I needed my head clear, so when I accepted the limply rolled cigarette, I held it between my teeth.

"What was the name of that Bruce Willis one?" he asked, casually.

"Which?"

"The abandoned one. Recently. Lee Grant was directing. It was a comedy. He was a boxer, or something. *The Battler*, or—"

"Something like that," I said. "*The Broadway Brawler*. In ninety-six."

"Right. Creative differences, they said. Or the one with Brando? And Johnny Depp and Debra Winger? They were already shooting in Ireland. In, like, ninety-five. Brando played a priest. The money dried up."

"Right."

"What was the name of that one? *Divine Rapture*?"

"Can't remember."

In honesty, the dope fumes were having an effect, inhaled or not. I wasn't used to it, and was starting to feel fuzzy. I handed the thing back to Johnny.

"It doesn't really matter now, does it?" I asked. "Because it's over."

I made this comment as pointed as I could. Johnny had no idea what I meant.

"Yeah, well. The film probably would have sucked, anyway."

"No, I mean this. This is over, Johnny," I said, trying to sound tough, feeling a little nauseated.

Sucking on the joint, dropping ash on the ground, Johnny just stared. "Huh?"

Hard-boiled indirection wasn't working. I cut to the chase.

"Why'd you steal my tape?"

"What tape?"

"And why'd you give it to Graus?"

Johnny just shook his head, perplexed. "I have no idea what you're talking about."

Speaking of trains, I suddenly began to fear I was on the wrong track.

"I've been trying to help you, Roy," he said. "It's not my fault that Graus is a temperamental old coot who's hard to get information from. He'll come through. Just relax."

As always, he sounded sincere. And, as always, there was something belligerent in his tone. Johnny flicked the joint away.

"Just relax," he said again. "And look at that view."

It sounded like an order. Besides the stations we were passing, the only things visible outside the train were occasional houselights. Still, not knowing exactly why, I began turning to check it out.

That was when he pushed me.

"Whoops," he said. "Sorry."

The train had lurched; he had barreled into me. It was clearly true, yet how much of it had been planned?

He and I were now near one of the chains, as the train began straightening itself out. Johnny held on to my shoulder to keep from falling.

"Okay," he said. "Crisis over."

We both could stand on our own. Johnny made as if to walk to the other side.

Then he turned and pushed me again, with both hands, hard.

I FLEW BACKWARD ONTO THE CHAIN, SCRAPING MY PALMS, HOLDING ON. Johnny leaped at me, turned me completely around with one swift move. Then, holding on to my belt, he tried to pull me down under the chain and shove me off.

"Hey!" I said.

Using my entire torso, I pushed against him. He went sailing backward, onto his can, sliding toward the other side. Now it was his turn to clutch a chain to hold on.

I glanced through the glass train doors, saw only commuters reading, talking, and sleeping. There would be no help forthcoming.

I grabbed one of the doors, tried frantically to pull it open. In a second, Johnny had regained his feet. He sank a fully formed fist into my kidneys. Then, impossibly fast, he did it again. The impact—it was like being kicked by a mule—threw me off the door onto my knees, and then onto my back.

Johnny was kicking at me now, the train rolling crazily to and fro. Laying his boots into my feet, thighs, and shins, he was directing me to the side. Flat on my back, I could be sent off the edge now with no problem.

My hands came up, to block the blows and catch his feet. Johnny kicked at my hands, sending dizzying pain into my palms and fingers. Undaunted, I held on to one of his ankles and turned.

Johnny slammed into the steel wall of the train, a few inches from the door. As if in a cartoon, he started to slide down, a second after impact. Then he remained, hunched in a pile. There was silence for a time.

"The only thing missing is the crutch," he murmured.

"What?"

"The crutch. You know. The guy's crutch."

I had a sudden flash. Fred MacMurray and Barbara Stanwyck. A moving train. Her husband had a crutch. They threw him off. *Double Indemnity.*

I was stunned. It was a new scene, or at least that's what Johnny would claim. Was it true?

Then I looked down.

Johnny's fall had sent the contents of his pockets onto the swiveling floor of the train gap. I saw a wallet, a pen, a ChapStick.

And the key to a car. A Honda.

The second I spied it, as if on cue, Johnny looked up at me. Still groggy, he was unaware of what he'd revealed. I bolted before he got wise.

With a great yank of the glass door, I barreled into the train. I ran through the rocking car, my crazy hair and sweaty face causing stares from the commuters.

Even pulling open our door didn't awaken Katie. She was dead to the world as I came, chest heaving, into the compartment.

"Wake up," I said.

After a second, she revealed her pretty blue eyes.

"What's up?" she said, squirming. Then, fuzzily, she saw my condition. "Oh, right. *Double Indemnity,* Johnny said. Graus is working. Was it fun?"

"Do you have money?" I asked, heatedly. "Give me the money you have."

Katie just looked at me, thrown. Then her confusion turned, ever so slowly, to fear. "What's the matter, Roy?"

What could I tell her? That, in different disguises, her boyfriend had been tailing me through three states and two continents? That I—and most likely she—had no idea who he really was?

I decided to skip specifics. My voice grew calm. I didn't like leaving Katie. But she, after all, had made her own bed.

"I need money to get home."

Even though she didn't understand, my tone made Katie nod. She quickly pulled a leather bag from the seat beside her.

"It has to be Johnny's, okay? I didn't bring any." Then she rifled through his stuff, bringing out a surprising number of American and Dutch bills and several handfuls of change. I jammed it all into my front and back pockets.

The train was slowing down. I looked out the door and saw Johnny limping determinedly down the aisle, heading our way. It seemed like a good time to get off.

"Look," I said. "Why don't you come with me? Get away from him?"

The idea seemed to interest, excite, and disturb Katie. She was, of course, a big fan of taking risks. But not the kind involved in leaving Johnny. I could see it in the way she shook her head.

"See you around then," I said.

This time, she nodded. The train came to a halt.

I stood on the platform, hidden among people, as the train pulled out again. I saw Johnny furiously scan the crowd for me from our compartment window. Appropriately, in the filtered glass, his features were almost indistinguishable.

PART 5
MAINE AND PHILADELPHIA

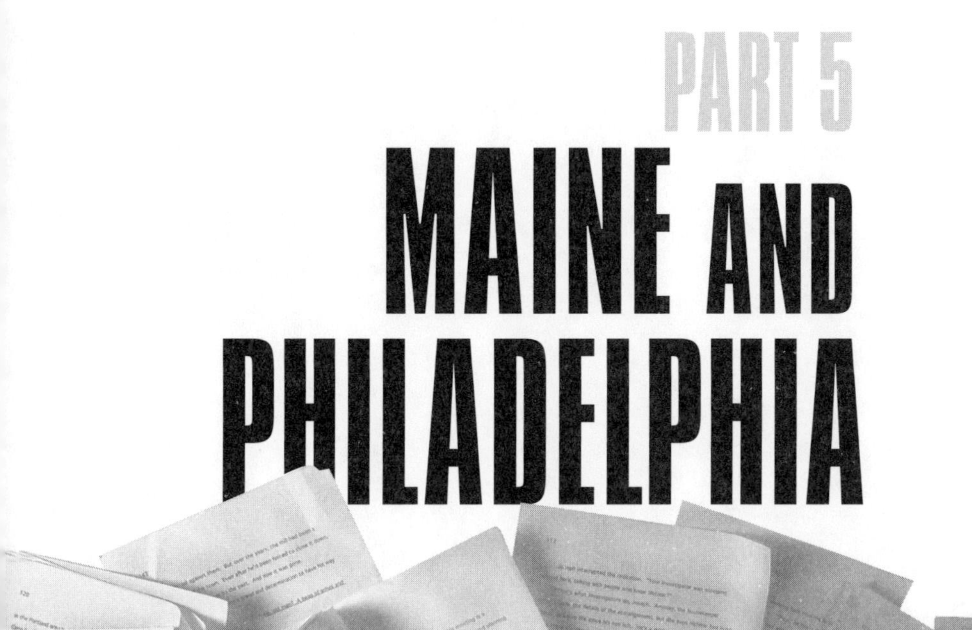

JOHNNY'S MONEY PAID FOR MY FLIGHT HOME.

I rode business class, to take advantage of his largesse. I read a free *Wall Street Journal* and actually found its entertainment page. There was one story of interest:

STUDIO BETS MILLIONS ON A QUIRKY "QUELMAN"

> Alan Boilerman, maker of acclaimed whimsical indie films about dysfunctional familes, has been handed his biggest studio assignment yet. It's a huge, multipart adaptation of the beloved cult dodeca-ology, *The Seven Ordeals of Quelman*. Boilerman plans to bring his trademark loony comic style to the project, adding and altering many elements of the fantasy. So far, he's received only thumbs-up from fan Web sites. . . .

No stalking or attacks for glamorous young directors, I thought. I almost felt sorry for Abner. Almost. I figured out how to fold the paper this time, and left it, in a tidy pile, on my seat.

Dena was staying on the water again.

This time, her house was only an apartment. It was located up a rickety exterior staircase that was attached to a bait store. It sat half a mile from the tacky main street of Bar Harbor, Maine, where T-shirts, kayak rentals, and lobster tchotchkes ruled. Still, the Sound was basically in her backyard, and it smelled better than an Amsterdam canal.

And she was glad to see me.

"I was worried," she said.

I was glad to see her, too. The red streak in her hair was now green. Otherwise, she looked the same, maybe a little thinner from anxiety. She wore a SpongeBob T-shirt over pants to a grandmother's suit.

Her father's one-bedroom had essentially been cleaned out. Only a few packed boxes remained, plus a mattress, a lamp, and a clock radio, all on the floor.

"I'm almost done here," she said. "They start showing it next week."

"And then you go back . . . where?" I realized I never knew where Dena lived, before she worked for Howie.

"I've sublet my place in Brooklyn," she said. "But I'll . . . I'll figure it out."

Never one for sentiment or disorder, she wouldn't be more expansive. Still, I could tell that uncertainty was weighing on her. And I only had more to offer.

"So this Johnny Cooper was the guy who's been following you? The other guy who got to my father's hotel before you?" she said, after I explained.

"Right. And this time he almost had me, too."

"How did he always know where you were?"

"Beats me." I stayed away from speculation. I was too wiped out from the long flight home.

"Do you think he thought my father's tape was *Clown*? And that's why he stole it from you?"

I smiled at her using the film's trivial nickname now. "I guess. And maybe he stashed it with Graus for safekeeping. He didn't know Graus would want to see some 'entertainment' with his maid friend."

"Maybe." Dena wasn't so sure.

"Sorry I lost it. I mean, you . . . you might have wanted more of your father's pictures of you. This time, in motion."

She shrugged, dismissing the letdown. "I've got enough."

There was a pause, as both of us slowly saw the dead end we had reached. I considered Johnny's cash in my pocket. I knew I should hold on to it, for my mother, and for anything else I might need. It was basically all I had. But, looking at Dena's weary face, I knew there were all kinds of responsibilities.

"Come on," I said. "Let's get a big, overpriced dinner."

We went to one of those lobster joints where you sit outside and eat as much fish, bread, and corn as you can fit into your face. In her own impassive way, Dena ate like someone who'd been starving. I'd only seen a Dorito's bag in her father's kitchen.

I tried to gorge as much as she. But something reduced my appetite. I realized that, even if I were done with the chase for the movie, someone else might not be.

And if Johnny Cooper had gotten as far as Europe, how hard was Bar Harbor, Maine?

I looked around the picnic area. I saw a family of three, two chubby adults with one fat, screaming kid. I saw a teenage couple, practically licking each other's faces. An elderly woman was sitting alone, sucking on a lobster leg.

"What are you looking at?"

"I'm not sure," I answered.

"You think he'd—"

"Well, why not?"

Dena had no reply. I saw a maintenance worker shaking out a garbage can. More kids. I looked past the restaurant grounds to the water it abutted. There were all kinds of boats docked there, from sailboats to yachts. Who knew who was on them?

"Well, if you're not going to eat this," Dena said, ever practical, "you ought to wrap it up."

My round robin of suspicion ended at our table. I saw Dena placing the rest of my dinner in a doggie bag. She was doing it carefully; she so clearly cared about me. I couldn't help it, I felt more disappointment about her father's tape than gratitude. And that didn't make me proud.

"Don't be silly," she said. "You can't go back to New York *tonight*."

I hadn't intended to. I was exhausted; I'd even hoped to stay a few days. But suddenly I felt that being alone again would help me think.

Besides, there was just the one mattress.

"All right," I said, weakly. "The floor will be fine."

"Now you're being infantile."

It was a statement of fact from Dena. Precise, businesslike, she pulled down the cover and sheet of her father's mattress and plumped the single pillow. Then she doused the light.

In the dark, I could see her start to undress, pulling her child's T-shirt up. Then we both turned away. As ever, it seemed weirdly instinctive for us to avoid anything else. I quickly stripped to my shorts and crawled into bed.

A wave of fatigue hit me as soon as I lay down. I barely felt Dena rock the mattress as she joined me.

"Good night," she said.

I smelled Dena's newly washed nightgown. I thought instead of Marthe's leotard, of Katie's freckles. Then I thought of trivia.

"Anne Bancroft replaced Patricia Neal in John Ford's *Seven Women,*" I said.

Dena didn't hear me. She was faced away, talking, too, but in a dream.

"Lost," she was saying. "Help me. I'm lost."

Wasn't it wrong to be displeased by a woman so displeased by herself? I reached over and wrapped an arm around her. Immediately, Dena held on. In a moment, she was quiet, and so was I. The only sound was a seal in the water outside.

At that moment, the world seemed uninhabited, except for a trivial man and a woman without a subject—or, more precisely, with a subject that had brought her only unhappiness.

The next morning, I called my machine in New York. I was shocked to hear Katie's voice.

"Roy," she said, breathlessly. "Get in touch with Leonard Friend in Philadelphia. Ask him about Chapter Fourteen. And tell him that I love him."

Suddenly, on the tape, in the background, I heard a door open. I heard Johnny's voice. Then, without another word, she hung up.

I SHOULD HAVE LET IT GO.

I mean, I no longer had a financial backer, except for an unwitting Johnny. I had family responsibilities and a newsletter to put out. But the trail that seemed to end had opened up again. And, at long last, it might lead me to *The Day the Clown Cried.*

Besides, I owed it to Dena.

"I took all that lobster meat out and put it in a sandwich," she said, handing me a paper bag the next morning. "There's one piece of cornbread left. The fries I had to chuck."

I didn't know what to say. I had a sense that we sort of loved each other, but in an incredibly muddled way. Why, given my life, should that have been a surprise?

"Thanks." It seemed an inadequate expression. I followed it up with a big hug, which Dena returned and took time to relinquish.

Finally releasing me, she said, "Be careful."

"Where will I be able to reach you?"

"I'll let you know. Check your machine or e-mail. Wherever there's someone unemployed, there I'll be."

I looked at her a second. It was an allusion to Henry Fonda's big speech in John Ford's *The Grapes of Wrath*: a joke and a movie reference, two firsts for Dena.

"John Ford was replaced as director on *Mr. Roberts* by Mervyn Leroy, though both got billing," I said. "Joshua Logan did some reshoots, too. He had directed the play."

While I was talking, Dena had been busy refolding the lunch bag in my hand. Only when I was finished did she meet my eyes again. I guess you can't have everything.

"See you, Roy."

"Right. See you."

My only contacts in Philadelphia were Claude and Alice Kripp. They were trivial people who had managed an impossible feat: They had gotten married *to each other* and procreated. I had bonded with their son, Orson—now seven, named after Welles—during my search for *Ambersons*. Today, I needed more of what they knew. In particular, who was Leonard Friend?

In their mid-forties, Claude and Alice had recently had a second, last-chance child, Ida, named after Lupino. Alice had retired from her job teaching film at Wellesley; Claude had taken a new post at the University of Pennsylvania. His campus office was filled with family photos, pipe smoke, and the warmth of domestic happiness.

As usual, Claude wished me to have some of it.

"I hope you'll have a home-cooked meal with us tonight," he said. "I know Orson would love to see you."

"That's nice. But I have to get back." I wasn't staying over; I'd stashed my stuff at the train station. Johnny's cash was fast disappearing.

"I'm so sorry about what happened with Jeanine," he said, referring to my *Ambersons* debacle. "There seemed to be a future for you two."

"Apparently not," I said, evasively.

"Yes, well, you know what they say about women and buses. Don't run after one, there'll always be another one right behind." Claude refilled his pipe, chuckling.

I never stopped marveling at Claude's unique combination of folksy normalcy and trivial knowledge. Most people could only manage one or the other. Like me, for example.

So, as usual, no matter how much I liked their kid, Claude's ode to sweet domesticity fell on deaf ears.

"Look, how can I reach Leonard Friend?" I said.

Claude stopped, surprised, mid-chuckle. Then he looked straight at me. "Leonard Friend? Why do you want to reach *him*?"

This was always the dangerous moment: How much should I share with other trivial people? I decided to skirt the central issue and dissemble. After all, if Katie "loved" this Leonard guy, how bad could he be? Then I thought of Johnny and Graus and felt unsure.

"I've been, you know, referred to him."

"You *have*?" Claude seemed revolted. "Well, far be it from me to judge, Roy, but . . . you *have*?"

Claude's reaction caused me to back off a bit. "Well, you know, not . . . referred, exactly . . . it's just a job thing."

"You're going to *work* for Leonard Friend?"

"All right, look—" What was the guy, a corrupt CEO or something? "It's not a job, exactly, it's . . . just research, I—"

"Look, I really shouldn't judge, but why would you want to research FamilyFlicks?"

I caught my breath. FamilyFlicks. It was a new group of self-appointed censors who cut nudity, violence, and foul language from current movies and then sold them on video. Studios and directors were trying to outlaw the practice, but until the lawsuits were settled, the organization continued its not-so-dirty work. Leonard Friend apparently was on their payroll.

"Well . . ." I was trying to think fast. "To be honest, I want to go undercover, do an exposé of them for my newsletter. But let's keep that between ourselves, okay?"

This did more than satisfy Claude. "Good for you! Now my world makes sense again. Okay, well, I think"—he was scrambling in a local phone book—"Yes—their office is on Walnut, off Spruce."

"Okay. Thanks." I started to rise, happy to be off the hook.

"You know how Leonard came to work at FamilyFlicks, don't you?"

This stopped me. "Well . . . tell me what *you* know."

"Leonard was working as an editor for a publishing house in New York. Alice and I once tried to sell him a book, *Precode for Kids: Films for the Whole Family, 1930–1933*. But he said it was too limited." Claude sniffed, clearly still annoyed. "Anyway, he had bought a history volume for their military imprint. About the Luftwaffe. And it was generally believed that the book was . . . so *he* must be . . . pro-Nazi."

"Is that right?"

"Yes. So, since the publisher had been bought by a German conglomerate, he was shown the door. Then I guess he decided, well, my cover's blown, why not really commit, you know? Hence FamilyFlicks."

Soon Claude was shaking his head, chuckling again. Before long, he began a new lecture on the joys of fatherhood and family. There was a very nice, recently widowed adjunct professor he wanted me to meet.

I thought of what I'd just been told. From Claude's chubby, ruddy face, I moved my eyes to a bookshelf above his head. There were dozens of film studies, from academic treatises to popular biographies. There was a history of religious imagery in the works of Harold Lloyd. There was Troy Kevlin's *The Boy-O Keeps Ringing the Bell!* and Howie Romaine's *Fatherhood Is No Joke*.

And there was *I Am Graus!*

I waited until after he gave me the available woman's phone number. Then I pointed vaguely to the books. "May I . . . ?"

"What? Oh"—Claude turned—"Sure. Anything you like. Just, you know, watch the bindings."

I opened Graus's profane memoir to the acknowledgments page. Among his self-serving thank-yous was one to his editor. It was just as I had suspected.

"Is this the, you know, uncensored edition?" I asked, casually.

Claude noticed which book I had chosen. "Of *Graus!*? No, no. Who on earth has that?"

I thought but didn't say: maybe Leonard Friend, that's who.

THEY MAY HAVE BEEN *FAMILY*-FRIENDLY, BUT THEY WEREN'T FRIENDLY.

That was the feeling I got as I sat in the FamilyFlicks waiting room. The place was around the corner from Philly's Avenue of the Arts, the reconstructed thoroughfare full of theaters and hotels. It was in a nondescript walkup above a Blimpie's on a street as yet ungentrified.

There was no name on the buzzer. The waiting room had only bland landscape paintings on the wall. A well-scrubbed young woman sat at the reception desk, as perky as she was steely.

"I called earlier," I said, for the third time.

"Oh, right." The girl checked me out, as if assessing if I were a lawyer, reporter, or another kind of troublemaker. She finally decided I was someone to ignore, not fear. "Let me try him again."

She apparently buzzed Leonard, waited endlessly, then whispered.

"Tell him Katie Emond sent me," I said, but she waved a discouraging finger at me.

There was more waiting and more whispering. I knew I was about to be given the heave-ho, so I opted for the obnoxious. I had only one piece of ammunition, and no idea how powerful it would be.

"Katie sent me!" I said, loud enough to permeate the receiver.

The girl gave me a furious look. Then, as I had hoped, she heard a new tune from Leonard. She hung up, then glared at me.

"He'll be with you in a minute," she said.

It was sooner than that. A paunchy, pasty-faced, balding guy of about forty-five stood in the doorway of the inner office.

"You know Katie?" he said.

Leonard Friend's office had even more of an uncharacterized quality as the rest of the place. His walls were, in fact, bare; a few nails and hooks in the wall attested to posters recently taken down.

"Excuse the minimalist look," he said. "We're switching our design scheme."

Hiding any evidence of the movies you're cutting T and A and exploding heads out of, I thought. But I only smiled.

Leonard smiled back. He had a nervous quality, and already seemed defensive, without my having said a word.

"Some people don't understand what we do here," he said quickly. "We're taking movies away from the cultural elite and giving them back to the people. It's the wave of the future. Malleable movies."

As he spoke, he was arranging papers on his desk. Something to keep his idle hands from being the devil's playthings, I thought.

"I hear you," I said, apparently not taking a side.

"It'll all become clear. It will be a crucial new kind of interactivity."

I thought of such hot potatoes as Billy Wilder's raunchy *Kiss Me, Stupid,* made in 1964. Ray Walston had replaced Peter Sellers. Leonard would have replaced a lot more.

"Must be a change from doing old-fashioned publishing," I said.

He stopped fiddling, and looked up. Instead of resenting my knowledge of his life, he seemed eager to relive old times. His tone became wistful. "Well, I had quite the experience there. I edited lots of movers and shakers. I was about to start editing the Olsen Twins when . . . things went south."

I nodded, again trying not to express an opinion. I couldn't know, of course, who else Leonard had worked with. And the one name I knew, he had conspicuously omitted.

"What about Graus Menzies?" I said.

There was a long pause. Then Leonard seemed to take it in stride.

"What about him?"

"Well—"

"And *how* do you know Katie?" His tone stopped at clarification on its way to suspicion.

"Just good friends."

"I see." Leonard seemed to find this improbable, given the man he was looking at.

"Well, I haven't seen her since I left my old job. She was in the publicity department. What exactly do you . . ."

"Chapter Fourteen."

Suddenly, Leonard stared at me, as if it had been a "trigger" and he was entranced. His hands started bunching and collating papers again, as if acting independently of him. "I see. And was Katie the one who—"

"She said you'd be able to help me."

Leonard's hands were moving even faster now, as if he were shuffling a giant deck of cards. He never stopped staring, weirdly, at me. "Well, I'm sorry, but I don't know why she would have . . . I mean, I don't know what she was referring to. . . ."

Leonard had now officially won the award for World's Worst Liar. He picked up his phone. In a cracking voice, he spoke like an untrained actor in a student film. "Marie? Is my two o'clock here?"

I tried not to laugh at the cliché. Leonard worked for people who sanitized movies others had made; there wasn't an original emotion in the place. And, I sensed, Leonard couldn't have handled it if he had one.

He couldn't handle it when he did.

"Katie said she loves you," I said.

It was another word to hypnotize him. He seemed to melt, his mouth dropping open, his hand releasing the phone. In this weird way, across an ocean, Katie and I were once again working in tandem.

I assumed that Leonard had become intolerant for the same reason many others do: a broken heart. I bet he had seen merit in that Luftwaffe book shortly after Katie turned him down.

His voice was thick. "Did she . . . tell you that?"

I nodded.

"Well, why doesn't she . . . tell me that herself?"

"She's shy."

I hoped my intention was clear. If Leonard let me read the chapter, Katie might be, shall we say, grateful. So what if it wasn't true? This was for a bigger cause than protecting the public from smut. This was for *Clown*.

"She's the only one I've ever shown it to," he said, thoughtfully.

For a second, I was confused—and repelled. Then I realized: He meant the *chapter*.

"Really?" I said. "Interesting."

"It wasn't even in the censored edition. It never went into the book at all."

"I see."

"What do you plan to do with it?"

"The right thing," I said, vaguely. "Don't worry."

Still a zombie, Leonard rose, very slowly, from his chair. He took a key chain from his pocket. He approached a file cabinet behind his desk. He started to open one of the drawers. Then, having second thoughts, he started to close it.

Right on my hand.

I had followed him there, not sure of his resolve. Now the two of us struggled for the small stack of paper inside.

"Where is she?" he asked, as I tried to yank out the drawer.

"Don't worry about that—"

"I think it's only fair that you tell me where—"

"I will, as soon as you—"

"Should I call the police?"

Leonard turned. The receptionist was standing in the doorway, looking cute—and pitiless.

"No," he said, wearily. "It's all right."

While he watched her leave, with one great pull, I got the drawer free. It flipped off its track, sending pages, bound with a rubber band in a plastic bag, all over the floor.

"Now look what you did," he said, seething.

He gripped both of my wrists with the full force of the unrequited. I felt a frightening pressure on my bones. Then, as if surrendering, he released me.

"Please, then," he said, "read it here."

CHAPTER 14

Sweden Spring 1972

I am a prisoner!

Not really—I'm no man's prisoner. But I've been hired to play one. It's not even a part. It's an extra job. For Jerry Lewis!

But no one can make Graus Menzies small. Let them try! I will bite them!

We're in Sweden, and I'm slogging along, in a concentration camp. When the camera picks me up, the world will see the true face of pain. I have prepared. I have dieted, I have stayed awake. I'm an artist. Let the editor dare to cut me out!

In truth, I am young, just thirty, and paying my dues. Greatness will come later. It is endless, tedious work. I suffer as much as anyone in history has. I feel familiar grumbling in my gut and my groin. I want to eat! I want to love! But first I must suffer for my art.

And for Jerry Lewis!

He plays a clown called Helmut Dorque (pronounced Dork),

I Am Graus!

sentenced to a prison camp for insulting a Nazi. We extras are political prisoners, brought into a separate area, bordered by barbed wire.

Today I am one of a few adults among children. We are looking through the barbed wire, at Jerry clowning on the other side. He wears a chalky face and charcoal on his lips. He salutes and knocks himself out. He "sews" with a hair from his head. He puts on a too-small jacket. His pants fall down.

We all laugh. I make sure to laugh the loudest of all. But the camera is not even on me.

Catching my attention is a little minx sitting on the set. She is called Elsa (not her real name). Does she work for the studio in Stockholm? I think so. I know she is a leggy young blonde with an insolent air. A princess. Yet she notices Graus, as he trudges back and forth, in agony.

When Jerry calls "cut," I am full of energy and at the woman's side. At first, she ignores me, her nose in the air. Yet she is intrigued by the filth on my face, the torment in my heart. She keeps looking at me. She knows I am a man who confers greatness on women.

"Shouldn't you be with the others?" she asks, haughtily.

"I'm not one of many," I say.

"But you're an extra."

"I am extra. There is more of me than of most men."

I can see a faint ripple go through her pale skin. I am no flatulent producer! I am a peasant! I am Graus! She feels the truth of this.

"I shouldn't even be seen speaking to you," she says.

"It will be our secret," I say. I place a card in her hand with the address of my Stockholm hotel. My hovel. Where the peons, the trash of the production are staying.

"What makes you think I would ever come to such a place?" she says.

205

She will have to climb through the mud and dirt to reach it. She will do it, if she wishes to be a woman.

"You have always wanted to be there," I tell her.

She knows it is true. But it is time to return to work. Jerry is calling.

That night, I wait. But I do not doubt. I know that, sooner or later, Elsa will descend to Graus's level. Smoking, I look out the window at the crappy street. I see a roach creep across my floor.

Then a taxicab pulls up.

I watch Elsa get out, demurely covered by a fur coat. Her feet are in black high heels. She carries a shiny purse. She has probably come from a fancy function. As the cab pulls away, she looks at her surroundings and shudders. Is it from fear or excitement?

Both!

I have switched on no light. I have left the door unlocked. I turn, as it creaks open. She stands there, lit only by a dim bulb hanging in the hall. Our eyes meet. Then she opens her fur.

She is dressed as a chambermaid.

My blood moves.

Without a word, she removes one high heel. Then, with it, she suddenly smashes out the hall bulb. Its fragments scatter to the floor. We are plunged into total darkness, where we both belong, where we are at home. Then she enters and shuts the door behind her.

Of course, I expect to be her master.

"I believe these shoes need shining!" I say, and point to my scuffed-up loafers.

She does not move. I clear my throat.

"I said, I believe these—"

"I heard you!" she yells at me, shocking me into silence.

I Am Graus!

I regroup, a bit—what's the stupid American expression?—thrown for a loop.

"That's no way to keep your job, cheeky young miss," I say.

Elsa only rolls her eyes. Then she starts marching around the rotten room, rubbing dust and blowing dirt from surfaces. Then she looks at me with a face of purest disgust.

"What a pig you are," she says.

"Excuse me?"

"Yes, you. You're scum, you know that?"

I can't believe my ears. This isn't the way this encounter is supposed to go. She is supposed to accept my supremacy and her own lowliness. Instead, she goes on and on, blaming me first for befouling the room—"Haven't you ever heard of a vacuum?"—and then for befouling everything on earth.

Something strange is going on.

Even though she is the maid, Elsa is turning the tables. Her gesture of subservience—wearing the costume—has given her the license not to serve. She is willing to be menial; that gives her the power to be superior. I don't understand it, either, but I find, to my amazement, that I like it.

Graus Menzies likes being insulted!

Elsa stops. She pushes me. I stumble back, stunned. I approach her again, puffing my chest out, daring her.

"Go on. Or haven't you got the guts?" I say.

This time, she slaps me right in the face.

The sensation is startling. My cheeks are on fire. But it's not the only thing reacting. I have become engorged.

Graus Menzies likes being beaten up!

Elsa has hidden a feather duster in her bag. She takes it out, waves it in my aching face. Then she turns it around and knocks me in the head with its handle.

207

I fall against the bed, dizzy and dazed. But I don't get up. I choose to stay down.

She takes another object from her seemingly bottomless purse. It is an old-fashioned paddle, the kind you use on naughty boys.

Graus buries his face in the nasty bedspread, his behind in the air. He closes his eyes.

Whack! Whack! Whack!

This is more pleasure than Graus has ever known! I am big enough, proud enough, to provoke such a punishment! The maid pummels her master until the sun comes up, until it's time to go back to work for Jerry Lewis. It is the greatest night of my life!

Later, before we leave, we sit on the bed, side by side, like children.

"How's your career going?" she asks, adjusting her apron.

"My what?"

"Your career, how is it—"

"How do you *think*?" I bellow, jerked back to real life. "I'm Concentration Camp Prisoner number three forty-eight in a Jerry Lewis movie! How do you *think* it's going? And what is Jerry doing, anyway? 'Dying is easy. Comedy is hard'—isn't that what they say?"

She didn't reply.

"I have no money, I have no agent—how do you *think* it's going?!"

I don't mean to scream at her, but it's a sore point. Why does a man of my caliber have to struggle so? It has set me off.

Elsa lets me rave on and on. She strokes my hair, compassionately. Then she pulls on my ears until I moan with excitement—and stop complaining.

"Maybe things will change now," she says.

I have no idea what she's talking about. It just seems like a thing one says. But there is no time to discuss it. I hastily agree. I beg her for one last good hard smack. Then I am off to Jerry and she is off . . . where?

I Am Graus!

She won't say. Elsa enters my disgusting bathroom. When she emerges, she has changed into a fetching sundress. The chambermaid is just a memory.

And what a memory it is! I keep Elsa in my mind as I slog through my final paces on the film. During lunch, I cannot sit down without wincing, then weeping, then smiling. The other extras stare at me. But I don't care! I flip them off. Let them get their own wonderful pain!

She never returns to the set. I hear a producer or some big shot complain about his errant girlfriend, who's left town without a word. It must be her.

But Elsa has been right. From that moment on, there is no more extra work for Graus. My talent and my legend only grow (see Chapters 15–27). There will be Wenders, Fassbinder, *Macaroon Heart* (with that hideous brat, Gratey McBride, who was dubbed by a dwarf).

Accepting myself, what I am, what I need, makes it possible for me to force other people to accept me, too. The realization makes me a finer actor. A bigger star. A better man.

I begin to re-create the original Elsa with other chambermaids. While it is usually good, it is never the same. I can never forget the woman who made me grovel and made me great.

Elsa doesn't forget, either. Years later, I am in Paris, staying in the best hotel, playing a leading role.

When I return to the hotel at night, there is a package waiting. No return address.

"Who left this?!" I demand of the mousy clerk who calls himself a man.

"A beautiful woman," he says. "She didn't give her name."

As if it's the finest heroin, I clutch the package to my breast. In my room, my fingers trembling, I rip it open.

209

It is a tape. A copy of all the footage shot on *The Day the Clown Cried.*

My eyes fill with tears. It is her way of remembering.

Over the years, the legend of Jerry Lewis's film has grown, as has Graus's. It has never been finished or released, only gossiped and dreamed about. I had read that the studio in Stockholm owned the negatives. Now Elsa has given me this priceless object as a gift.

I know it would be a windfall, but I have no interest in making money from it. I will never give it up. Telling no one, I will take it with me wherever I go. It will matter to me only as a memento of that wonderful woman, of that first spanking hand.

It may have been the day the clown cried. But it was also the day Graus Menzies cried *out*—in wonderful, unforgettable agony, truly, for the first time: "I am Graus!"

"NO ONE ELSE HAS EVER SEEN THIS?" I SAID, EXCITEDLY, LAYING DOWN THE last page.

Watching me read, Leonard Friend had gone from shuffling papers to flipping a pen in the air. Now, startled, he sent it sailing behind a cabinet.

"What? Oh, no," he said, bending to recover it. "Except for . . . well, you know. Katie."

"And why didn't you include it in the book? Afraid you'd be arrested for knowing about a stolen film?"

Leonard shook his head. "Graus changed his mind. Actually, that's putting it mildly. He demanded I give him the pages back. He swore me to secrecy. Then he . . . head-butted me." Leonard pointed to a small scar in his left temple, one that I hadn't noticed. "You would think he meant to keep it secret so he could sell the film himself. But he really had . . . as you can see . . . sentimental reasons."

Leonard sighed, as if reflecting on his own. At least Graus wasn't being mercenary in hoarding the film; I almost respected him for it. Almost. And Leonard had been equally moony in holding on to the chapter.

"But still you . . . disobeyed him and kept it?"

"I had had a Xerox made. I . . ." Leonard was actually perspiring. "I thought it might impress Katie."

"And did it?"

The dissipated man seemed relieved to finally unburden himself. "No. She didn't care much. That's why I was frightened when she went to work for Graus. I was sure she'd tell him, and he'd come looking for me and kill me. But I guess she never said a word."

No, but casually, at some point, she must've told Johnny, I thought. Someone who *was* willing to kill for it.

"You won't . . . reveal . . . where you got this?" he asked, suddenly frightened.

"Don't worry, no."

He relaxed again. "Good. Now, if you don't have any more questions . . . you might give me the information I asked for. Where is Katie?"

Leonard's tone had changed from the pathetic to the slightly threatening. It reminded me that his mission in life wasn't benign, that he used his grudges to deprive others. It made me suspect that I couldn't stall him forever.

Luckily, I didn't have to.

Behind me, I heard someone enter the office. I turned and saw the pert secretary again. She avoided my eyes completely and looked only at Leonard.

"I'm afraid I went ahead," she said.

For a second, the guy didn't understand. Then, surprised, he checked out his window. In the street below, a cop car was pulling up.

I had gotten what she meant right away. Immediately, I had risen. Instinctively, I still held the chapter.

"You idiot!" Leonard yelled at her, face crimson.

I bolted from the room, pushing harshly past the girl. Then I powered my way through the waiting room and out into the hall. As I left, I distinctively heard the intercom buzzer going off. The cops were in the building.

I avoided the elevator, the *down* arrow of which already shone. Instead I flew into the stairwell, slowing my pace as I started downstairs.

I had been on the third floor. Now, beneath me, I heard someone coming up.

What did I have to be afraid of? I wasn't sure. Then I felt the chapter in my arms and understood. If I had arrived innocent, I was no longer.

The footsteps were coming closer, only one flight away. Reaching the second floor, I only hoped the stairwell door was open.

It was. I slipped through it, finding myself on a bland hall in the small office building. I stood to the side of the door, hoping whoever was on the stairs—and I assumed it was a cop—hadn't heard me come or go.

After a sweaty second, the feet passed by and continued up.

I disappeared back into the stairs and quietly took the last two flights. I emerged from the building, the chapter rolled and held inconspicuously in my hand.

I turned onto the Avenue of the Arts, and tried to get lost in the lunchtime crowd. I hoped I could make the walk to Thirtieth Street Station without being stopped. It was in Leonard Friend's interest, I knew, to keep the cops at bay. His organization teetered on the edge of illegality and would soon, I bet, be pushed over by irate filmmakers.

But, maybe by stealing from him, I was only being interactive.

Johnny paid for my ride back to New York. On the train, I thought about what I'd learned.

Graus had been planning to watch *Clown,* not porn, that day with his newest chambermaid. Johnny had replaced Graus's copy of *Clown* with what he thought was mine. Then the young filmmaker tried to kill me. Graus would be next to go, and then Johnny would have the picture all to himself.

Now it seemed that Katie, troubled by my escape, had come to truly fear Johnny and had called to help me out.

None of it explained how Johnny knew all of this, his presence at Troy Kevlin's house or anywhere else. The story was becoming clearer but wasn't yet clear.

I only knew that, if I could reach Graus through Katie, I might save the old actor's life. I could also see his copy of *The Day the Clown Cried.* When it came to finding films, none of us was altruistic.

It seemed like a simple plan. Thinking of it gave me energy as the train pulled into New York. I headed from Penn Station to my apartment. A big Hollywood movie was being shot in Times Square, and I sidestepped officious, self-important assistants with good humor.

Bounding up my familiar cement staircase, the steps and walls covered with graffiti, I couldn't deny it: I was happy to be home.

Then I opened my door.

Katie was standing there. She'd obviously been crying for a long time.

"Roy," she said, "Graus Menzies is dead."

PART 6

NEW YORK CITY

I DIDN'T KNOW WHAT TO ADDRESS FIRST: KATIE'S INFORMATION, HER PRESence in my apartment, or the condition of my apartment, which was a sty. I noticed that Katie had moved a huge stack of my newsletters from the only available chair. If only she'd given me a "head up," as Marthe might have said, I could have cleaned.

I decided to start with the most obvious question. "What are you doing here?"

"I told your super I was your cousin," she said, sniffling. "He let me in."

My ancient super was a fool for a pretty face, breast, or behind. I thought I was getting a big extended family, starting with my cousin Dena at Howie's house. Still, this was an incomplete answer.

Katie seemed to waver on her feet; I guided her into the empty chair. I brought her some water in my only clean glass. As she drank, pulling out of the faint, I thought that Fred MacMurray had replaced Paul Douglas in *The Apartment,* and Kim Novak had replaced Vera Miles in *Vertigo.*

"I meant, what are you doing in America?"

Katie nodded. "Oh. We're filming here. In Times Square. Graus was shot in Amsterdam. This is when he was still alive."

I was confused for a second, then realized she meant: as the Nazi, in the movie. Going backward was customary in moviemaking; it caused trouble in real life.

"Johnny came with us. I tried to leave him behind, after Amsterdam, but he was so dogged. He scared me. That's when I, you know, called you. Did you get my message?"

"Yes."

"Did you see poor old Leonard—"

"Yes."

I bent to retrieve the chapter in my bag, as Katie paused to sip more water. Then she stopped me, her words coming in a rush.

"We're staying in a hotel near here. The day's work was done. Johnny suggested a new movie scene. I didn't want to play anymore, but how could I say no? Johnny said we'd re-create *Psycho*. Graus was still down the hall, in his own room.

"Johnny and I started with the bra scene. You know, at the beginning? Where Janet Leigh and John Gavin are having the affair? So the two of us were on the bed."

I couldn't help but blush a bit, imagining it. As ever, Katie was unembarrassed. As she spoke, hurriedly, she pulled her hair back and tied it with a rubber band. She looked particularly lithe and freckled. I glanced away, to change my focus.

"We were, you know, starting to canoodle, or whatever. Then there was a knock at the door. Johnny got up to open it. Graus was standing there, in the doorway. It took me a minute to recognize him."

Katie paused, inhaling more fluid. She had piqued my interest and I felt impatient.

"Why?"

"He was wearing a woman's wig and a dress. I figured he had stolen it from wardrobe. He stood there, with this strange look on his face. I could smell he'd been drinking and toking. 'I'm Tony!' he yelled. Then he slammed the door behind him."

I was starting to get the picture, and my confusion and desire were turning into dread. I placed a hand on Katie's, and her fingers intertwined with mine, gratefully.

"Graus came closer, and his face looked so weird under all that blond hair. He reached us at the bed. I couldn't help it, I was afraid. In a second, Johnny was standing. He put his hand into his pocket. Then he pulled out that little knife he carries and put it in my hand.

"Graus came at me so quickly that I raised it, and . . . he ran onto the blade. He fell on the floor, and . . ." Katie faltered for a second. Then, gripping my hand tighter, she continued. "I looked at Johnny. He said, 'It was him or you. Graus said "Tony"—he was Tony Perkins. He would have stabbed you, like the shower scene. Didn't you see his eyes? He was nuts.'

"As horrified as I was, I was sure that he was right. I bent down and tended to Graus, lying on the floor, with his wig all funny. He was whispering something. I put my ear right next to his mouth, and then I heard it. 'Curtis!' he was saying. 'I'm Tony *Curtis*!' "

Katie looked at me, sure I would understand. And if I didn't, who would?

"*Some Like it Hot,*" I said, and Katie buried her face in her hands. "He was in drag, from *that* movie. And Tony Curtis was married to Janet Leigh at the time."

Her face still hidden, Katie was nodding, helplessly. When she looked up, she was weeping again. "He was confused. He was confused."

I nodded. "Poor Graus."

The actor must have been addled ever since he lost his tape. And poor Katie, I thought. Johnny had her do his dirty work for him.

I bet he was long gone by now. He didn't need me anymore; I didn't have the movie. Johnny was holding Graus's copy of *Clown,* and Katie was holding the bag.

In other words, I believed her story.

"Tell me," I said, "who registered at the hotel?"

"Johnny had me do it. He said he couldn't find his credit card."

I sighed, having anticipated that answer. "So, what did you do . . . after, I mean, Graus?"

"I just ran. We both did, in different directions. Though I called nine-one-one, in case Graus wasn't, you know, so dead."

She said it with the hopefulness of a child. Katie was in over her head, as she was when she encountered any aspect of real life. Working for a living, dying—these things were no fun at all, so no use to her.

"I didn't know where to go. So I called information and got your name," she said. "I knew I could depend on you, Roy."

Using my hand, she pulled herself up, leaned forward, and kissed me on the cheek. Someone found me dependable. Even if I spent most of my life in a movie dream, compared to Katie, I was an adult. My mother would have been surprised to hear it.

Katie started to cry again. I poured her a stronger drink this time, from a bottle of Francis Ford Coppola's wine someone had given me as a gift. It had been sitting for months, uncorked and unfinished, in my kitchen.

Tasting it, Katie made a face. "Maybe we should go out and get something better. Are there any good bars in your neighborhood?"

I almost laughed. "I don't think you're getting the seriousness of this. I mean, this is really—"

"Oh, I don't want to talk about it anymore," she said, petulantly. "I'm tired of it. Okay?"

I shrugged. "I guess."

Katie shook her head then; it was the closest I'd ever seen her come to despair. "I've made an awful mess of things. Johnny was no one to trust, though he was exciting, in a dangerous sort of way. And Graus . . . I never slept with him, you know, no matter what people think. I bashed him in the head with a Kleenex box once, because he begged me to. But I like tenderness, myself."

The whole time she was talking, she stayed close to me; so many smells came from her. I liked all of them, but she wrinkled her nose.

"Can I take a shower? I'm funky."

"So's my shower."

"I don't mind. Really."

"Let me just, you know, use a sponge."

It had been a while since someone nontrivial had been in my bathroom; our standards for cleanliness are different. But Katie was refreshingly unconcerned.

"That's fine, that's fine," she said, starting to run the shower. "It's spotless, it's great."

I backed off, sponge in hand. The hot water looked inviting; I was rank, too, from traveling to Philadelphia. But I started to leave the room.

"Hey, Roy?"

"Yes?"

"What's this?"

Katie now wore only a T-shirt and light blue panties, which clashed with her red pubic hair. She was pointing to her pale, freckled belly, which her shirt didn't cover. There was a curious dark splotch near her navel, clutched by a little ring.

"Is it blood?"

"I don't know. I can't tell."

"Really? Well, why don't you come closer?"

She gently guided me to my knees. It was obviously a birthmark; she'd had it for years. I played along. It wasn't so easy to say you were lonely and afraid and wanted somebody; I knew that better than most.

Softly, I placed my hand on the spot. Then I placed my lips on it.

Her stomach was warm. The skin beneath her waistband was warmer. Katie slowly stepped out of her panties. I started to pull my shirt up, over my head. Steam filled the air.

"Whatever it is," I said, "I'll wash it away."

"I BROUGHT BACK YOUR TAPE," SHE SAID LATER.

For a second, half-asleep, I had no idea what Katie meant. Then I remembered: Dena's father's tape.

"Graus practically threw it at Johnny and me," she said, quietly. "You know, when he was still alive."

I smiled to myself, brushing her hair a little. Hours earlier, dripping wet, we had shifted to my bed from the shower. My drain had been clogged, and water had risen as high as our shins. But both of us had been very clean and felt very close when we moved to the foldout couch. We were still damp, and I stuck to Katie now as I kissed her.

"How long have we been sleeping?" she asked, squinting at the light.

"I have no idea." I picked my watch up from the floor. "Six hours."

"Jeez." Katie stretched a little. "I feel good, though."

So did I. Recalling our circumstances didn't spoil my mood; it enhanced it. Katie felt secure with me, and I didn't mean to let her down.

If her affection had been motivated by accidentally murdering someone, who was I to complain? Anyway, I liked her.

But the reality of the situation was dawning on her now, too.

"I wonder what's happened."

"I'll tell you in a second," I said.

It was a glorified studio, so I couldn't go far. But, considerately, I kept the TV volume low, as I surfed channels for news of Graus's death.

Eventually, I found some. An esoteric European actor with one Hollywood hit twenty-five years ago didn't top any reports. But a murder was a murder.

Some tape of Graus in *Macaroon Heart* was shown. A "female companion" was being sought. No name was mentioned; the cops were keeping it to themselves, I guessed. The part about Graus dying in a dress would come out sooner or later, too, on the Internet, if nowhere else.

I switched the thing off. Then I turned. Katie was lying with a pillow over her face, to stop the sound. Feeling lousy, I returned to her.

"Okay," I said. "That's all."

Katie uncovered her face.

"All of this over some movie," she said. "I don't even like Jerry Lewis."

"No? Have you ever seen *The Nutty Professor*?"

"With Eddie Murphy? Just the sequel. Why?"

"Never mind."

There was no point in explaining. Katie hadn't cared when Leonard Friend showed her Graus's chapter, and she wouldn't care now.

"Are you hungry?" I asked.

She nodded.

I kissed her forehead. "Don't answer the door or the phone."

"Sesame or poppy, okay? And butter, no margarine."

Even as I was smiling, I was aware that Katie had never been prepared for anything. That had been her charm, and now it was her downfall.

Holding a brown deli bag, I stood outside the glitzy Times Square Marriott Hotel, where Graus's story had so abruptly ended. Crime scene tape was already sagging on the front doors; tourists and other gawkers were starting to thin out. Everyone was moving on. For most people, after all, Graus was just a guy who played Nazis. A few cops, however, still hung around.

Looking up, I was distracted by something. A huge new billboard featured Marthe in a repeat of her old ocelot campaign. This time, though, she was selling a sciatica pill from the conglomerate that owned the perfume. At least she was bringing in some cash for the taxes, I thought. Then I gazed back down at the street.

Standing near a patrolman was Detective Florent.

Why was everything always in his precinct? This was what happened when you lived near "the crossroads of the world"; I made a mental note to move.

At the moment, however, it was too late.

"Hey!" he shouted. "You!"

He'd been whispering to a cop; I bet he was saying something like, "There's that loser I'm always running into."

Then he was in my face.

"What the hell are *you* doing here?"

"It's a free country," I said, brilliantly, and tried to get by.

"How come when there's something bad, you're always around?" Florent seemed genuinely confused.

"See, you're a cop. You're *only* around when something bad is happening. I'm around when good things are happening, too. But you're not there." This had the makings of a decent joke, but it was too long-winded. Florent didn't get it, and it only made him angrier.

"Don't give me that. Tell me what—"

"Look, I heard about it on the radio," I said, to mollify him. "I just thought I'd take a look. I'm a movie fan, remember?"

Florent stopped for a second. Then his cheesily handsome features shifted. "Hey, Graus Menzies was an extra in *The Day the Clown Cried,* wasn't he?"

I was getting out of there. His trivial qualifications were growing by the encounter, and it worried me.

"Wasn't he?" he shouted, now in the distance.

I barged into my apartment suddenly enough to startle Katie. Dressed in T-shirt and shorts, she was sitting up, against the bed's pillows, clicker in hand. She pressed it to mute.

"Wow," she said. "You scared me."

"Sorry." I was agitatedly handing her the deli goods.

"Look. He's dancing on the ceiling, like in that Lionel Richie video."

I glanced at the classics movie channel, LCM. Fred Astaire was doing his famous number from *Royal Wedding*.

"That was copied from *this*," I said, curtly. "And Jane Powell replaced Judy Garland who replaced June Allyson."

"Know-it-all." Katie was peeking at her bagel in its wrapper. "Hey, I said sesame or poppy, and this is whole whea—"

"Just eat it, for chrissake!" I found myself screaming at her.

There was a long pause. Katie looked hurt. She rewrapped the bagel very, very slowly. She pressed the mute button again. Fred could be heard tapping on the wall.

"If I want to be yelled at, I'd go back to Graus," she said, softly. "Oh, wait a minute . . ." Then her bottom lip began to tremble.

Beaten by her childlike quality, I sat down beside her. "Look, Katie. I can't guarantee your safety here. The cops could show up, any minute. We've got to figure out what to . . ."

Katie was nuzzling at me now. In another second she was kissing me, gently, all over my neck. Another man could have resisted this obvious attempt at diversion. But another man might have had more women in his apartment recently. Besides, as I mentioned, I liked Katie.

"Mute it again," I whispered.

When we woke up, *Royal Wedding* had ended, and the station was showing an old short from the thirties where dogs played all the parts. A bulldog judge was sentencing a poodle prisoner to death. Silly as it was, it gave me a chill.

"It's nicer with you than with Johnny," Katie was murmuring. "He was never really *there*, you know."

I took the compliment, but a police siren cut short my pleasure. Only when it faded did I relax back into the pillow.

Katie kept complaining about Johnny, and I looked as much as listened. Left with only her T-shirt, she leaned languidly against the pillow. She looked like Vivien Leigh in *Gone With the Wind* after Clark Gable carried her up the stairs. Only, you know, without pants.

Suddenly, my mind raced, as if toward an answer. George Cukor was replaced by Victor Fleming as director of *Gone With the Wind* . . . Fleming directed *The Wizard of Oz*, in which Jack Haley replaced Buddy Ebsen . . .

"And Johnny always did things for the worst reasons. You've at least got a real passion, Roy. . . ."

Dudley Moore replaced John Malkovich in *Crazy People* . . . George Segal was replaced by Moore in *10* . . . and twenty years later, Segal replaced Moore in *The Mirror Has Two Faces*. . . .

"Johnny just talked about how much money he could make off trivial stuff . . ." She started teasing my foot with her own, ready to go again.

Barbra Streisand replaced Lisa Eichhorn in *All Night Long* . . . Eichhorn starred in *Yanks* with Richard Gere, who replaced John Travolta in *American Gigolo*. . . . Recently, Travolta was starring in a film co-starring Isabelle Adjani and directed by Roman Polanski, which was scuttled over "creative differences," even as Steve Martin prepared to take over the lead. It was to be an adaptation of Dostoyevky's *The Double*.

". . . and Johnny had a nose job, did you know that? I mean, what's with that? He wasn't an actor, he was a director . . ."

Someone who was *Gone With the Wind* . . . who had *Two Faces* or was a *Double* . . . and had something to do with a *10* . . .

I quickly sat up, yanked my pants from the floor, where I'd flung them. I scrambled in the pockets, for the last vestiges of Johnny's cash, which had paid for Katie's breakfast.

"Hey, what are you doing?"

Dollar bills flew out and were thrown aside. It was the change I was after. A quarter and a nickel rolled onto my rug. Then, at long last, so did another one of Johnny's coins.

A fake dime.

JOHNNY COOPER WAS STANLEY LAGER.

Suddenly it made sense—his changing identities, his violence, his immoral motives. Whether it was *Quelman* or *Clown,* who else would stalk someone so greedily over trivial things? How he'd trailed me, I didn't know. But if there were patches left in the picture, it was more complete than it had ever been.

Now all I had to do was find him. Then I could see the film and clear Katie. Was that the order of importance? I couldn't say.

"Where are you going?" Katie asked.

"I can't explain now. Please just do what I ask you. . . ."

I warned Katie again about going out. I told her not to answer the door, not even for the cops. I told her where the spaghetti was. I said I'd be back as soon as possible. Then I took money from her for transportation. We kissed, sloppily, before I could pull away.

I didn't say I was going a hundred miles from there, to the privileged upstate enclave where Stanley Lager hid. Jeff Losson had told me in his comic book store—could it only have been weeks ago?

Then, before I left, I removed the gun from my underwear drawer.

Three hours later, I was in Millwood, New York, standing on line at a bakery. There was a middle-aged man ahead of me, endlessly grilling the teenage clerk about the filling of croissants.

"Is there cherry? No cherry? That's too bad, I really like cherry. What else do I like . . . ? How about almond? No almond?"

Tension was causing a tremor in my eyelid. I tried to be inconspicuous among the well-heeled Dutchess County clientele, shopping for weekend brunch. But I could sense their uneasy glances at the grungy interloper in their midst. Who else had come to town by bus?

I was in Nature's Meal, the flagship store of the boutique bakery that had brought its goods to the Farmer's Market in Manhattan. It was the only place I knew in the community, where the answers to so many questions now might lie.

My turn finally came. Though the challah looked good, I was about to walk away.

"You need another job?"

It could have been no one else. I turned and, big, blond, sunburned, and contemptuous, there was the person I was seeking: Annabelle the farmer.

"No," I said. "I need something else."

We sat at a table in the back of the crowded store. Annabelle had agreed to "two seconds" of conversation, since she was "actually working here."

I didn't know where to begin. So much had changed since I held my balloon in Union Square. Yet to her I seemed the same rootless loser, not a determined detective on the brink of a breakthrough.

"Jerry Lewis's *what*?" she said.

I sensed this was the wrong way to begin. Annabelle the farmer probably hadn't seen a movie in fifteen years.

"He's a comedian, and this was his famous, unreleased serious—"

"Look, subway boy, I'm not a farmer, you know. I manage a bakery. I own a VCR and I actually get cable. I have a husband and two kids. I just never heard of this *particular* goddamn Jerry Lewis movie."

I took an uneasy sip of my coffee—Kona blend, and not on the house. I had thought she was an actual farmer.

"Not everyone has heard of it," I said, quietly. "It's a special kind of . . . this really doesn't matter. What matters is, there's a guy who . . ."

I soon stopped. If Annabelle didn't get *The Day the Clown Cried,* she'd never get Stanley Lager. So I skipped right to the most accessible matter at hand.

"Look, I need to find a mansion. It's around here. I think FDR lived in it. Now they have tours. But it's run-down. And somebody rents out one of its rooms, like . . . Rapunzel, or something."

Annabelle's voice, which had been irritated, now became exasperated. "For God's sake . . ."

"You have no idea what I'm talking about?" I'd get Jeff Losson for this. What did he know, anyway? He spent his life in comic books.

"FDR didn't live there. His *cousin* did. Take the West Side Highway occasionally, why don't you?"

Slowly, I felt a buzz of hope mix with the caffeine.

ANNABELLE GAVE ME A RIDE.

I sat in the back of her truck, crushed between bags of rolls and doughnuts. I arrived, smelling of pastry, just in time for the last tour at Steilerman, the mansion. She said nothing as I got out, but placed a cruller, wrapped in plastic, in my back pants pocket.

"I need your help in the city," she said. "So don't get killed."

Annabelle actually cared, sort of, in her own way. Seeing her little crinkly smile, I got out.

Soon I was taking the tour of the huge old house. Sweating, I walked behind noisy tourists, dressed in unbecoming shorts, and their stultified teenage children, who made lewd remarks and punched each other. Our tour guide was a retired volunteer, a man of seventy, who knew way too much about the home's former inhabitants.

"FDR's fifth cousin, Mr. Steilerman was a volunteer fireman and a voracious reader. This chair, bought in 1906 and stuffed with duck feathers and horsehair, was where he spent many an evening. He would often place both his feet on this ottoman. . . ."

If this was trivia, it interested a very tiny crowd. The Gilded Age joint was in blatant disrepair and, for every preserved piece of furniture, one stood fraying or collapsed. Entire rooms were roped off, as were staircases. Signs requested donations and desperately promised perks for members, like summer parties or bonnets for kids. I saw bowls overflowing with the fake dimes.

"Excuse me?" I said, interrupting our guide. "What's up those stairs? The ones cordoned off?"

The old guy stopped, in mid-description of the ottoman. Then, sighing, he just went on. "In those days, dinners often featured a glaze of mint jelly. They were served in the next room, if you'll follow me . . ."

"Is it true that someone lives in the—"

Now I was totally ignored by my host and shot contemptuous glances by my fellow guests. The little band proceeded into a dining room, where a long table had been set, with ceramic replicas of glazed jellies.

I made sure to stay behind.

I moved toward a staircase and sneaked silently over its velvet rope. The steps were soft and unstable; I crept up, giving them only the slightest pressure. I remembered that Kate Reid had replaced Kim Stanley in the film of Edward Albee's *A Delicate Balance.*

The staircase was a narrow funnel that probably led to an unpresentable past. I had a flash of Gratey McBride, and I instinctively raised a hand, as protection. But I made it safely to the second floor.

It was obviously decrepit, and undergoing an overhaul. Rooms were filled with ladders and drop cloths; walls were half-painted and plaster half-restored. I tiptoed past workmen, who gave me not a second glance.

Then I saw the security guard.

He was no spring chicken. He only had a flashlight; I at least had a fake gun. Still, I picked up my pace, and tried to walk inconspicuously by.

"Excuse me?"

I pretended not to hear, so intent was I in studying light fixtures and ceiling beams.

"Can I help you?"

He had caught up with me. I played the history buff, even though, of course, most of my information came from movies.

"What was this, the maid's quarters?" I wondered.

We both looked into a tiny room, with just a bed, a dresser, and a bowl for water.

The guy was forced to follow me. "Look, fella, you can't be up here. You've got to go back down—"

"And which was the pantry?" I tried to think of last-century words. "And the paddock? Where was the—"

"Sorry, but I don't know what—"

Then, over his shoulder, down the hall, I saw a door slowly open. A man emerged, his back to us. He started walking quickly away.

"Who's that?" I asked.

"Him? Oh, the guy renting a—look, buddy, that's it, let's—"

He'd said enough. The other man swiveled his head, swiftly, once, to check us out.

It wasn't Johnny—I mean, it wasn't Stanley.

But that didn't faze me. I shot past the security guard.

"Where are you—" he yelled. "Come back here!"

I started running toward the figure. I believed that I recognized him. That was because I had made one last stop before exiting the city.

Taylor Weinrod had been surprised to see me. I had arrived, out-of-breath, after leaving Katie ensconced at my place. I noticed that his fancy Riverside Drive apartment seemed virtually unchanged, though it now housed one less occupant.

Taylor was, as always, impeccably dressed, and looked every inch the executive at LCM. You'd never know he'd once been a trivial man himself in Jersey City, in long-ago days he preferred to forget. And of which I was a somewhat irksome reminder.

"How can I help you, Roy?" he asked, tersely.

He clearly thought I was looking for work—or that I had another trivial find to deprive him and his station of, as I had with *Ambersons.* But I was after something else today.

"I was wondering if you knew where I could find Abner," I said.

Taylor stiffened, noticeably. He'd left his wife and kid for our mutual friend, even wrangled him an on-air gig. But their affair had apparently been too hot not to cool down.

"You know that we've . . . called it a day?" In his successful-guy way, he tried to be discreet.

"Yes, and my condolences on that." I secretly thought I should offer congratulations. "But you're the only one I could think of to ask."

"Well," he gave an absurdist laugh, "I don't have his forwarding address, if that's what you—"

"Yes, that's sort of what I was looking for, to be honest."

I was hoping Taylor was just holding back, out of propriety.

"Well, would it be possible to send him a message, or—"

"No, for chrissake, Roy, it wouldn't!"

Taylor would never have raised his voice this way at work. I figured his guilt at dumping Abner—and how could it have been otherwise?—must have been great.

Still, his conscience would heal. I needed to know if Abner had been having any more trouble from Stanley Lager.

"Look," I said, "we're all adults. And maybe there's something in this for you."

I was gambling that Taylor would trust me again in a business capacity. It was worth a shot, though I was offering goods I didn't possess.

"It's about Jerry Lewis's *The Day the Clown Cried.* Maybe you and LCM might be interested in—"

To my shock, I saw that, never mind not believing me, Taylor didn't care. He gave a great, disgusted sigh. Then he pulled me, very roughly, to a nearby computer table.

"I want to show you something," he said.

As we waited for his machine to boot up, Taylor now talked with surprising directness. "You take a risk for someone, you change your life around for someone, and you get a big foot in the face for it."

Taylor had logged onto Abner's PRINTIT!.com. But instead of gossip or reviews, the screen now showed a video stream of what looked like real, spectacularly bloody surgery.

"Abner told me he was in the hospital for gout," Taylor went on, choking up. "But he was really having one of those . . . fat removals—those operations where they take out half your stomach, like that Beach Boys daughter had—" Carnie Wilson. "He even posted the whole thing on his Web site, for his fans. For God's sake, look at that!"

As the surgeon sawed and stapled, I looked away.

"He wanted to do it for his new hottie. He met him at a party. This guy, whom he never named, said there was no reason not to look the way you wanted, that there were wonderful things you could do for yourself with surgery now, and . . . what kind of person would *say* that?!"

Suddenly I thought I knew what kind of person. Tears were flowing freely out of Taylor's eyes. I felt sympathy for him. I felt shock that Abner, not *he,* had called it off. But, mostly, I felt a sense of urgency.

"So, *no,* Roy," Taylor spat out, "I don't know where you can reach him—"

"That's okay," I said. "I think I do."

And with a pat on his back, I was gone.

Now, the man on the second floor of the crumbling mansion picked up his pace. He fled into a room at the far end of the hall. It would only take a second for me to reach it.

I slowed down, aware there could be danger.

I knew the guy was Abner. And I didn't think he'd be alone.

RICHARD BURTON AND ROBERT MITCHUM TEAMED UP FOR A FILM THAT WAS abandoned in 1974. It was directed by Terence Young of *Dr. No* fame. Its title was what I felt I'd now hit: the *Jackpot*.

Abner tried to close the door on me, but I pushed it with full force. He offered little resistance. He just moved quickly beside Johnny/Stanley, who stood steps away in the tiny room.

"Nice try, guys," I said.

It was a maid's quarters, identical to the one I'd recently seen. The two men looked weirdly out of place in it, each wearing modern sweaters and slacks.

Johnny/Stanley was unchanged from how he'd last appeared in Amsterdam. Abner, though, had already suffered a reverse of the effects of his operation: He looked maybe fifty pounds heavier.

"Shut the door," Stanley/Johnny said.

I turned and saw the guard, who had stopped in the doorway. He gave a befuddled wave to the mansion's tenant, did as he was told, and disappeared.

When I turned back, the men were having predictable reactions. Stanley was smiling, smugly, and Abner was sweating, nervously. I directed my attention to the weaker of the two.

"Thanks for playing me for a fool, Abner," I said.

"I don't know what you're talking about," he replied.

"Come on, Milano," Stanley scoffed. "You're used to it. You've been a fool your whole life."

"Maybe. But it's better than being a psycho. *Stan.*"

Calling him a nut and by his real name unnerved Stanley. His little smile faded. Then, a second later, it reappeared, with less pleasure.

"I'm not the one chasing after a movie just so I can *see* it," he said. "*That's* really crazy."

"Well, I'm sure you've got your own plans for *Clown.*"

"If I did, it would be called eBay."

"Bastard."

The word just jumped out of me. I knew Stanley's motives were purely mercenary, but it hurt to hear it so baldly. I switched my sights back to Abner.

"He wasn't trying to kill you to preserve the integrity of *The Seven Ordeals of Quelman,* was he, Abner? He didn't even care. It was just an arrangement the two of you made after you . . . got together."

Abner twitched a bit, guiltily. Then he tried to recapture his old obnoxious self. "Yeah, right. Tell me another."

"You thought if you staged your own stalking, the suits at the studio would stop changing *Quelman*'s story. And you were right. Though, maybe your pal here went a little overboard on the knife wounds."

Chased by the truth, Abner started to move backward, slowly. Soon he was literally hiding behind Stanley.

"I was just a little frosting on the cake," I continued. "But you like frosting, don't you, Abner? Because once I told you I was going after *Clown,* and you knew my every move, you had Stanley follow me. First to the flophouse—where he scared an old man to death and found nothing—then to the Hamptons and L.A. From there, in Amsterdam, he could handle me on his own." I looked at Abner's protector now. I used an old movie line. "Too bad you didn't kill me when you had the chance."

"Why," Stanley laughed, "because you're going to do it now?"

I wanted to, of course. But I'd never done anything close to that. Besides, Stanley would know the gun I carried was a fake. He had used it to shoot at Abner in the diner.

So I threw the useless weapon on the floor between us.

"Taylor might want that back," I told my old pal. "He says hello, by the way."

Abner blushed, deeply. I almost felt bad for him then. He had fallen for a chameleon who expressed all our worst impulses. The dark side is a powerful draw for a trivial man.

And for other people, too.

"Katie gives you her best," I said, to Stanley.

Blushing wasn't in Stanley's palette. He only shrugged. "I haven't seen her recently."

"I have."

This surprised him, though he did his best to hide it. If I knew how Graus had died, he sensed the stakes were getting higher. He moved to force things to a climax.

"Well, if you haven't come to kill me," he said, "why *are* you here? To turn me in?"

This had occurred to me, of course. Doing so would clear Katie. But it wasn't my only reason for showing up.

"First," I said, "I want the movie."

Stanley grinned—very, very slowly. His features, so altered by surgery, had always been vague. Now, smiling more broadly than I'd ever seen him, he looked like what he was: a death's head.

He turned, swiftly. Then he reached beneath the thin mattress on the maid's old bed. When he faced me again, he held an object that the setting sun made sparkle like a bar of gold.

"Come and get it," he said.

FOR A SECOND, I DIDN'T MOVE.

Stanley had shown himself to be ferocious, hammering me and other people into submission. Still, this might be my last chance to have *Clown—and* deprive him of it. Both things were important.

So, again, I directed my attention to a man more easily defeated.

"Abner," I said, "think about what you're doing."

"What?" he said, clueless. "What am I doing?"

"I know it's tempting. He's promised you so much. That's important for guys like us. But use your head for a second."

"Why would I want to do that?" Abner actually said.

"You're depending on a person who's never been loyal to anything or anyone. You've served your purpose. He'll be on to someone else the minute he moves the merchandise."

Slowly, Abner seemed to get it. "This is different—hey, how would you know anything about it, Milano? You just sleep with your clicker at night."

I was sensing the cracks in Abner's ego. "Why be so desperate? Relax. Men are like buses, they . . ." Unfortunately, I forgot the rest of Claude

Kripp's folksy homily. "Look, one day, you might actually find someone who would be a fan of *Clown,* and not its pimp."

"Shut up, Milano," Stanley snapped. "This isn't going to work."

He was wrong; it was starting to. I could see Abner darting little looks at Graus's tape, held in Stanley's hand. It may have been cruel to play on his insecurities, but he had lost his victim status by being so ambitious. And the power of the powerless was a dangerous thing.

"Face it," Stanley continued. "You're afraid to fight me. So you're preying on the weak."

This was true, so I had no comeback. Luckily, I didn't need one.

"What do you mean, the weak? Who's weak?" Abner said.

I would let this one just play itself out.

"I didn't mean weak," Stanley said, irritated. "You know what I mean."

"No, I don't. Who's weak?"

Two things were happening. Abner was looking ever more greedily at the tape. And Stanley was losing his grip on it, the more he lost his temper.

"Forget it. Forget I said anything."

"I'm not going to forget it, I—"

"You're letting Milano play with your head. What's the matter with you, are you stupid?"

"Oh, now I'm stupid, too, not just weak."

It was working better than I could have dreamed. Stanley, so adept at stealing, punching, and shooting, was lousy at personal relationships. But then, why should he be any different from the rest of us?

"Let's just talk about this later, okay?" he said.

"No, I think we should talk about it now."

"Well, I don't agree, I'm sorry."

"I don't care if you're sorry."

Stanley had no intention of doing this anymore. He noticed the same thing I had: Abner had moved from behind him to before him. Near me.

That meant there were now two people within grabbing distance of the tape.

There were also two people to get through to reach the door.

So, ever resourceful, Stanley decided to spring a surprise.

He went out the window.

It was a narrow aperture, apparently all a maid in 1906 required. Stanley was slender, but had had the benefits of mid-century nutrition. So it took him a second to struggle through the space.

First, he had to hold on to the wood of the frame, which was frail, dirty, and full of chipped paint. Then he had to shove up the shaky bottom window. Then he had to squeeze himself out onto the ledge.

He only had two hands. And one of them was holding the tape.

In a second, Abner had poached it.

Halfway out, Stanley looked back, shocked at his boyfriend's audacity and speed. He glanced at me, enraged. Then, shaking his head with disgust, he fled the room altogether.

There was silence for a second. Abner's expression told me to let him go. But it wasn't enough to stop Stanley from having the film. I had to stop Stanley.

So I went after him.

LESS AGILE THAN STANLEY, I SMASHED MY HEAD INTO THE OPEN BOTTOM window. Cursing, I opted for legs first. Before I knew it, I had both feet on the thin ledge. Then, holding on to the shaking window wood, I snaked my top half out.

Immediately, I realized I had made a big mistake. Inside, catching Stanley had seemed a noble purpose. Outside, it was an act of insanity.

Stanley was a few feet away, balanced on the ledge, above the mansion's back grounds. He was moving, steadying himself by holding on to passing windows or grooves pitted into the building by time. All things considered, he was doing pretty well.

He turned back and saw me. He even had the wherewithal to laugh.

"You're kidding me!" he yelled.

I couldn't blame him. Hanging on to the maid's room window, I was shaking like a palsied old man, my face frozen in a smile of fear. My only thoughts: Marlon Brando replaced Anthony Franciosa in *The Fugitive Kind*; forty years later, James Woods replaced Brando in *Scary Movie 2*.

Stanley taunted me. "Don't look down!"

Of course, I did.

It was only two flights, but, a hundred years ago, they made buildings with less and higher floors. It seemed like that, anyway: many miles to the ground. On the huge back lawn, I saw the tiny guide continuing his tour, directing his group's attention to some topiary.

"It was here that Mr. Steilerman used his walking stick . . ." I heard him faintly say.

There was no way I could catch up. Stanley was skittering like a cat burglar now, getting the hang, before I could move an inch.

Then I heard a pleasant sound.

On another day, it would have been unnerving. But, at that moment, the creaking and cracking of an old home's ledge was a lovely woman's song.

The place was falling apart, after all. That was why they'd taken him in as a tenant in the first place.

Stanley stopped. Slowly, he looked beneath him, at the area of support now starting to collapse. He was like the coyote in the Warner's cartoons, a trivia area that wasn't really my own.

"Aw, no," Stanley said.

The tour group glanced up at the noise. They heard a man curse, shrilly. Then, the very next instant, Stanley and a small slab of concrete had cascaded down to join them.

I DIDN'T WAIT UNTIL HE HIT THE GROUND.

Gratefully, I clawed and angled my way back inside the window. Stanley might survive the fall but he'd be hobbled. That gave me time for some unfinished business.

I was lucky that I returned when I did.

The minute my feet hit the maid's room floor, I saw Abner at the door. He was almost gone, clumsily gripping a plastic bag, the tape sticking stupidly out of it.

"Where do you think you're going?" I panted.

Abner turned back. Then he closed the door. The color red had trouble covering his entire face.

"Nowhere," he said, innocently.

Abner was an adaptable guy, but he hadn't made the greatest career moves. He had blown his on-air LCM gig by cheating on Taylor. He had been fired from writing *Quelman* for, well, having no talent. And he had alienated himself from the human race by hooking up with Stanley Lager.

But he could always go back to being king of the trivial. And what better way than with *Clown*?

"We had a deal."

"I told you in my e-mail, Milano," he said, awkwardly, "that that was null and void."

"Well, why don't you get one of your fancy Hollywood friends to renegotiate it then?"

Abner sighed. This option was lost to him now, as were all of his industry contacts. Our correspondence wasn't worth the e-mails they'd been written with.

"I'll take it under advisement," he said.

That was the end of our attempt at civilized interaction. Both of us now tensed, prepared to return to the jungle.

"Give me that tape."

"Make me."

"I will."

"Well, what are you waiting for?"

Then we stopped.

"Hey!" a small voice cried. "Hey!"

Abner and I both moved, quickly, to the window. There, on the back lawn, the tour guide and his guests had suffered the results of Stanley's sudden landing. A few tourists were splayed on the grass, unhurt but stunned. Laughing, their teenage offspring were slapping each other's palms. A piece of ledge rested near them. The guide was yelling to no one in particular.

"He got away!"

I sighed. Being the trivial rat he was, Stanley Lager had once more scurried to safety.

"Well, I hope you're satis—" I started to say.

Abner didn't let me finish. He hit me in the back of the head with a porcelain water bowl, the room's only accoutrement. A turn-of-the-century artifact, it shattered, lessening its impact on my skull, but spraying sharp pieces into the air.

I turned, swiftly, my head sore and starting to bleed. Abner ducked from the shards zinging past his own face. This made him lose his balance; I didn't even have to push him to the floor.

He landed on his plastic bag, the tape both breaking his fall and punching him in the stomach. I stood over him, wincing from pain, relieved that he was beating himself up.

Instinctively, Abner rolled off the object stuck in his solar plexus, exposing the bag and the cassette inside. I reached down to pull it toward me. But Abner kicked it away before I could.

The tape went sailing under the vintage bed, hitting the wall it stood against. Like the steel ball in pinball, it immediately ricocheted back into the room.

"Good going," I said, rubbing my head.

Again, I bent to retrieve the tape. But, still flat on his back, Abner kicked it again, now sending it sliding near an ancient chest of drawers.

"You're going to break it!" I said.

"If I can't have it, nobody will!"

Abner sounded like the crazy villain in an old sci-fi serial. Still wincing, I laughed as I stooped to get the tape.

I didn't laugh for long.

With both feet, Abner got me in a scissors hold around my ankles. Shifting suddenly, he snapped me toward the floor. I grabbed hold of the old dresser, but it was a bad idea. The shaky furnishing crashed down with me.

The wooden chest headed directly for the prone Abner. He rolled away at the last minute, and it smashed onto the floor, directly between us. I heard a hundred years' worth of wood crunch and collapse. I was only glad the maid wasn't alive to see it.

Now Abner was an old Western villain. He leaned up over the chest to see me, using it like a barricade in a barroom gunfight. I jabbed a fist at him, but he darted back behind it. I waited to see his face again. In a second, he reappeared. I punched again; he dodged.

"Abner," I said, "this is getting ridiculous."

So I directed my attention elsewhere.

The tape was lying past our feet, as if it had fled to safety from the falling chest. I didn't know whether, preoccupied with me, Abner had noticed.

If I scrunched down too low to be seen, using the dresser as a shield, I might be able to crawl and reach it. Then I could stand, run, and hit the door before Abner.

I flipped slowly around, so my head was pointing toward the cassette. Crawling like a soldier, all elbows and knees, I began my silent journey toward it. I might have made it, too.

Except that Abner had the same idea.

I met him there, both our heads poking out beyond the chest at the same time. Our eyes locked. Then our hands began to reach.

The tape was achingly beyond our grasp. Our fingers strained to touch it. The digits were like little tired runners, trying to cross a finish line. We were equally determined, neither one falling away.

But only one of us had recently had surgery.

"Oh, no!" Abner said and stopped. "My staples!"

I kept reaching. In one second, *Clown* was mine.

But I didn't even have time to celebrate.

"What's going on in here?"

Both of us looked up. The security guard was standing in the doorway.

I LEFT HIM TO ABNER.

One look at the fake gun on the floor froze the guy where he was. Holding the tape protectively, I scooted past him and out the door. I only caught a brief glimpse of the guard waving at me, threateningly, with his flashlight.

By the time Abner found his feet, I figured, I'd be safely out the front door. But once I'd accomplished that—escaping through the main entrance right as the CLOSED sign was being posted—I had another problem. What to do now?

A local sheriff's car stood in the mansion driveway. A traumatized tourist was recounting his ordeal—Stanley and the ledge—to a bemused cop. I took a deep breath. I slowed my pace and ambled like a normal guest, albeit a sweaty and bleeding one. I made it by before anyone could ask a question.

Then I walked a little faster. I saw another vehicle parked a few feet away. It had been waiting.

"Just so you know, I'm not taking you to New York," Annabelle said, starting her truck.

"That's okay," I said, sitting again amid her buns. "The bus station will be fine."

I had considered asking if Annabelle might offer me a hayloft, or a hammock, or wherever rural people slept. But getting back had to be my priority. The overnight bus ride would give me time, at last, to relax.

Once onboard, any relief that having the *Clown* afforded me was shortlived. I had bought the next day's *Times* and opened it to the Metro section.

ASSISTANT SOUGHT IN ACTOR'S MURDER

Police are looking to question Katherine Emond, a personal assistant, in the apparent slaying of actor Graus Menzies. Emond, 29, had been staying in the same hotel as Menzies while he shot the movie *Beach Head* in Manhattan. The sixty-two-year-old actor was found dead of a stab wound in his room on Wednesday night. He was best known in America for his role in the 1976 comedy-drama *Macaroon Heart,* co-starring Gratey McBride . . .

Beneath the story was a photo of Katie, which looked like it came from her high school yearbook. She'd hardly aged in the interim—mentally or physically—and would be easy to recognize.

What was the good of getting the world's second-most-coveted film if I was an accomplice to murder? With Graus's tape in my possession, I even had a motive.

And, as I may have mentioned, I liked Katie. I only hoped she had stayed inside.

Outside was more dangerous than I had even imagined. When I reached the city and turned the corner on my block, I saw something that chilled my blood.

A police car. Double-parked outside my house.

It was unmarked, but if you'd lived in town as long as I, you start to recognize them. Maybe it was the red bubble light sitting, less than inconspicuously, on the dash.

Sneaking by a cop in Manhattan was a lot harder than in sleepy upstate. Especially when it was Detective Florent.

He was leaning against the car, staring off, finishing a smoke. I immediately lowered my head, turned around, and started retracing my steps. I crushed a shopping bag carrying breakfast for Katie—and, not incidentally, the cassette—against my chest.

"Hey! You!"

The corner had been so close, only two steps away. But there was no point in running for it now.

I froze. I remembered that James Cagney had replaced Spencer Tracy in Robert Wise's *Tribute to a Bad Man.* Composing myself, I swiveled slowly around. I reminded myself to be as boring as possible. Something told me that would be the easy part.

"Yes?"

We stood at a standoff, with almost a full block between us. Florent didn't stop slouching against the car. After a second, he moved the smallest amount possible. He twitched his second finger at me.

I had no choice but to obey. As I approached, he got into the driver's seat. I flashed a quick glance up at my apartment window. Obscured by the fire escape, a woman stood there, watching. Then I got in the car beside him.

FLORENT LOCKED ALL THE DOORS.

"Welcome home."

I swallowed down what was now a very dry throat. How long had he been waiting? He seemed to be sporting stubble.

"Thanks."

"Somehow I knew it would lead back to you."

I had the terrible suspicion that rattling off geeky sentiments wouldn't distract Florent today. His Central Casting cop face had never looked more serious or, interestingly, less handsome.

"Movies are nice," he said, "but real life is a little bit more serious."

"I beg to differ," I couldn't help replying.

I saw Florent grimace, as if he were restraining himself from smacking me.

"But maybe," I said, quietly, "that's a discussion for another day."

Too annoyed to speak, the detective just pushed a poorly Xeroxed photograph at me. It was of Katie, the high school one.

"You know her, right? Let's not waste time."

I held the picture at an appreciable distance, as if trying to focus far-sighted eyes. I squinted, stalling for as long as I could.

"Now, let me see . . ."

"Because she's been seen around here."

"You don't say . . ."

I was roiling inside. As I'd feared, Katie had been fidgety and wandered. It was her wont.

"We do have informants, you know. All over this crappy neighborhood."

"Well, it's a lot better than it used to be," I said. "There are some nice restaurants now. And they're building that new apartment house that—"

He talked over me. "When I rang your bell, your cousin told me there was nobody else there. But it won't take long for me to get a warrant. Don't you want to avoid that?"

My cousin? Had he met Katie? Was the picture not that good a likeness? Or had she gone out to get hair dye, or something? This time, I didn't have to fake my confusion.

"I really don't know what you're—"

"Look." Florent leaned so close I could tell he'd just used one of those mouthwash strips. "Maybe this act fools all your midnight-movie, trivia chatroom, blow-up-doll-loving friends. But you're playing in a whole other league now."

I had no idea how real the threat was. Search warrants were items from cop movies to me. He was right that I was now deep inside an unfamiliar place: real life.

Katie's future was in my hands. For the first time since this whole thing began, I felt truly helpless. And no amount of filmdom facts and figures would ease my pain.

"Look, if you put out," Florent said, either impressed by my obdurateness or suddenly showing mercy, "there's no reason for you to have to be involved."

The plot was getting thicker. If I gave Katie up, *Clown* and I could go scot-free. What wasn't clear was how that made me feel.

In the space of a second I had to know myself better than I ever had.

I was like a computer trying to find a file, when the title of every document and program on its hard drive flashes by on its screen. I had to scan myself to see if I could find my priorities.

I hardly knew Katie, after all. And I'd been looking for *Clown* for a long, long time.

"Well, Milano? What's it going to be?"

Swallowing deeply a final time, I made up my mind.

"Uh . . . well, here's what I can do for you . . ."

I didn't complete my sentence.

I just placed my shopping bag into Florent's hands.

He looked at me a second, baffled. He rustled inside the bag. Then he looked back at me, incensed.

"A sesame bagel? What the hell do I want with *that*?"

"No, no, for God's sake," I impatiently searched for him now, "it's *this*." I jammed the tape into his grubby hands. *"The Day the Clown Cried."*

Florent was silent. He just sat there, holding it.

"Be the first on your block," I said.

The detective still didn't speak. I started, ever so slowly, to sweat.

Florent had, of course, correctly characterized my sorry acquaintances. But he had at least professed to have a common interest with them. How deep, I wondered, did it go?

To my horror, was this about to be recorded as just the weirdest bribe in New York City history?

Then I had my answer. Tears of gratitude were forming in Florent's eyes.

Some people yearn to be powerful, others to be truly trivial.

"Go on," he said, his voice choked with emotion. "Get out of here."

ALL I KNEW WAS: KATIE BETTER BE GRATEFUL.

That was what I muttered to myself, as I made the climb up my lousy stairs. She better know how much I had sacrificed. She better straighten up. She better start to live a different kind of life. Because people don't get the world's second-most-coveted lost film every day. And people who do don't give it up.

The bitter words were about to spring from my mouth as I stabbed the key into my door and shoved it open.

The only hitch was: Katie wasn't standing there.

Dena was.

"Oh, Christ," I blurted out. "Of course."

She was my cousin, too.

"I'm glad you're here," she said.

Dena looked better fed and rested than when I'd left her in Maine. The streak in her hair—had it last been green or red?—was gone. She was left with her natural shade, a mousy brown. She wore a simple, smocklike dress that suited her own age. It seemed to be her attempt to be an actual adult. I thought she looked better the other way.

She gave me a hug, one that was conspicuously short-lived.

"I lied to your super, and he let me in."

"I'm sure he did."

"By the way, some guy came to the door, snooping around. He didn't say he was a cop, but I got the feeling that he was."

"You were right."

Exhausted, I found my way to my one chair and sat. I noticed the place had been straightened up.

"You really didn't have to clean," I said.

"There wasn't much else to do. What happened to your head?"

For a second, I didn't understand. Then Dena touched a tender spot on my scalp, which showed the mark of Abner's bowl assault. Typically, Florent hadn't even mentioned it.

"I got hit by a . . . never mind."

"Are you all right?"

"No."

Actually, I felt okay, physically. It was just the regret, fury, and disappointment that hurt.

Then I looked up. "What are you doing here, anyway? And where's . . ." I cut myself off, before mentioning Katie. Was she gone for good? No one else was there, but the bathroom door was closed.

"I came here to . . ." Dena paused, uneasily. Then she started to pace, displaying an uncharacteristic case of nerves. "I broke my lease in Brooklyn. I decided to move into my father's apartment in Maine myself."

"You did?"

"Yes. I got a job at the local bookstore. It'll pay the bills until I figure out something better. And I came here to, well, to see if you wanted . . . to move in with me."

I stared at her. Dena was still walking, not meeting my eyes. She was trying to make this confession with her usual businesslike tone, but it was tough. "But then, when I showed up, I saw that . . . that wasn't a good idea."

Before I had time to understand, the bathroom door opened. Katie emerged. She looked fresh-faced and alert, none the worse for wear.

"Hi, Roy," she said. "What happened to your head?"

"See," Dena said, "she answered the door."

ALL AT ONCE, THERE WERE SO MANY THINGS TO DIGEST. MY FIRST RESPONSE was anger: I had told Katie not to go out *or* let anyone in. Then I realized it no longer mattered. And Katie would never understand what I'd done for her, anyway.

So I was free to absorb Dena's main point. She had wanted the two of us to be together. But seeing that I was with Katie ended her plan.

Should it have? I didn't even know. Did what I felt for one cancel what I felt for the other? And what about the *Clown* that had broken my heart?

"Here," I said, and handed Katie the shopping bag. Now it only held, of course, her snack.

"Thanks," she said, checking it out. "But Dena and I already ate."

"Oh."

Katie gave me back the bag. Suddenly ravenous, I started to bolt down the food myself. It was the only thing that made sense to do.

"You've got some cool friends," Katie said, and the two women smiled at each other. "Dena has been very sympathetic about my, you know, plight."

Not surprisingly, Katie had been loquacious, revealing her crime to a virtual stranger. Dena and Katie had bonded, and maybe that was predictable, too. One was a responsible parent, the other a restless kid.

"Look," I said to Dena. "Maybe we ought to talk about all of this."

"We don't have to. I'm heading back." She had returned to her usual practicality, and seemed comfortable there.

"Well, maybe you don't have to, I—"

"I do have to, though."

"But maybe you don't have to go back *alone*."

"No, I do."

There was a finality about the statement that stopped me. It would take true romantic conviction to challenge it, and I wasn't sure I felt it. My next remark surprised everyone.

"No, I mean . . . take Katie with you."

It's painful to learn that one sacrifice often leads to another. Better to get them over with all at once, I thought.

"She's safe this minute. But we shouldn't push our luck. It'd be best for her to hang out in Maine for a while."

A general silence fell over the small apartment. Dena looked at me, quizzically, and then at Katie. I turned to Katie, too, to gauge the level of hurt feelings.

She didn't have any. As always, she was just intrigued by a new possibility.

"You think?" she said.

"Yes," I replied.

"Well," Katie said. "I *do* like lobster."

I shot a look back at Dena, to see if the feeling was mutual. She seemed open, yet still undecided.

"It'll take some time for things to die down," I told her. "But Katie's case is closed. See, the cops wanted *Clown* more than her."

Dena's eyes grew wide. "You mean you actually got—"

"Don't remind me."

"And then you gave it—"

"Yes, yes. That's enough, stop."

Dena gave a low whistle through her open mouth, something I didn't know she could do.

"Well," she said, "I *could* use someone to split the driving."

"Great," Katie chirped. "I'll go pack my stuff."

My place being a hovel, she went to a corner, while Dena and I continued, in lowered voices.

"I found out who saw your father," I said, "who scared him to death. And who came after me."

"Really? Is he—"

"Yes," I lied. "Now he's, you know, he's in custody."

"Wow. This . . . this is all so impressive, Roy." Dena looked at me with a new expression on her face. I think it was respect, but I hadn't ever seen it enough to know.

"But I guess we'll never know why your dad called me in the first place."

Dena didn't answer. Katie joined her at the door, a canvas bag slung over her shoulder.

"Okay," she said. "I'm good to go."

"Here," Dena said to her, going in her own bag. "Wear this kerchief. At least until we get out of town."

Katie happily covered her head in a do-rag way. That, plus her freckles, made her look like a tomboy character in an old comic strip. I still liked her, I couldn't help it. So I glanced away.

Then Dena gave me something, too.

"Well, I *know* why my father called you," she said.

It was her father's tape. The one Dena had sent me. The one Katie brought back from Graus to me.

"And once you watch this, Roy," she added, "you'll know that I'm not leaving because I don't love you."

"What? But—"

The two women were out the door before I could finish.

"Bye, Roy!" I heard Katie say, faintly, from the stairs. "Thanks for everything!"

Slowly, I closed the door. The place was quiet then. I heard only the drip of my broken bathroom faucet. I expelled a long sigh of exhaustion.

Standing there alone, I had a strange inkling that I would never see Katie again. But I would see Dena. What had she meant?

I took the tape over to my VCR.

AUNT RUBY WAS RELIEVED THAT I HAD COME.

She didn't say it, of course. Far be it from her to evince a sentimental emotion. I could feel it in the way she hugged me when I walked in the door.

It was a week later. My childhood home was filled with boxes. The place had been put on the market; there was a lot of packing and cleaning to do.

"There's nothing to drink, except water," Ruby said, ever the nurse. "But that's all anybody ever really needs, anyway."

"No, thanks. I'm fine."

My mother wasn't dead. The medical bills had grown so great that her house was the victim. My mother was going to stay with her sister until she could move into assisted living. She'd be a quiet guest; she still had yet to say a word.

Aunt Ruby would have held me responsible for this disaster. But when I called, I'd given her hope that I had found a remedy. And hope had, surprisingly, given her a new vulnerability.

"So, Roy," she said, her voice quivering a little, "what's the good word?"

"I'm not sure yet," I answered. "But it'll help if you give me a little . . . space."

I had a small window of opportunity in which to exploit Aunt Ruby's trust, and I used it. Nodding, obediently, she backed off. I knew she'd return to form soon—with downbeat wisdom and new demands—so I had to work fast.

I walked up the stairs, to my mother's room.

As I climbed, I thought about the tape I'd watched in my apartment. With Dena and Katie gone, I'd wavered for a while, afraid to put it in the VCR. Then I thought: Why avoid watching Dena's father's secret movies of her as a kid? What was there to fear? So I popped it in.

It wasn't footage of Dena.

It was another abandoned movie.

It starred me.

It was footage of me as a child, taken from a safe and timid distance, just as Dena's had been. It was the truth that Ted Savitch had wanted to tell me when I showed up at his flophouse. He had lured me with *Clown,* knowing that I'd respond.

I reached my mother's room. She lay in bed, surfing channels, her eyes alert, a lunch tray empty on her bedside table. I knocked, lightly, on her open door.

"Mom?"

She turned to see me. Then her face lit up. With mute excitement, she waved me over. I came forward, but only so far, stopping at the foot of her bed.

"I think I know what this is all about," I said.

Seeing the look in my eyes, my mother immediately recoiled. Then, slowly, she began to cry, in silence. The tears seemed as much from relief as unhappiness.

Ted Savitch had met her that day at the double feature in Times Square. It was one of her secret movie outings in the city. His e-mail address had been Ted6569, the day and year I was secretly conceived. No wonder Dena and I had always been drawn to, then repelled by, each other.

"Ted Savitch was my father, right?" I said.

He was another replaced actor.

My mother didn't respond. She just kept crying, making no noise.

"Let me guess," I said. "He recently got in touch with you. He was in bad health, his heart was failing. He wanted to connect with you before he died. To make dying easy. I don't know the details. But you know what I'm saying."

The specifics didn't matter. They had been lost in his missing diary pages. What mattered was that she'd probably felt closer to Ted in one day than she ever did to the man she married. There was a life she had never pursued, a life that linked all three of us: Mom, my real Dad, and me.

"See," I said, "he got in touch with me, too."

I was quiet then. I'd done all the talking, the explaining she couldn't do in the weeks that she'd been mute.

Slowly, then, small moans began to come from her. They grew louder, breaking the embargo on discourse that had lasted until now.

She nodded. Then, at long last, she spoke. She said what she always did to me. This time, it wasn't a way to goad or upbraid me about my life. It was a question about herself, one my mother wished desperately to have answered.

"What do you do," she said, "with a thing like that?"

EPILOGUE

GRATEY MCBRIDE WAS LIFTING HER OSCAR AGAIN.

This time, though, it was in triumph. Now in rehab, she was being interviewed on LCM by Taylor Weinrod, before a showing of *Macaroon Heart*. Looking pretty and dressed presentably, she had brought her award along and held it proudly, not aggressively.

I was cruising channels, preparing the new issue of *Trivial Man*, which was late by weeks now. There would be no mention of *The Day the Clown Cried*; I couldn't afford to blow the bargain I had made with Florent. Still, I sensed, in the admiring and resentful eyes of my little community, that word of my latest gain and loss was leaking out. It was bound to make me even more of a hero and a pariah than I already was.

How did I feel about that? I was part of a real family now, not just one made up by the trivial brotherhood. The former was profound and forever; the latter was sillier, safer, and asked much less of me. Which one did I prefer? I didn't yet know.

It had already had a positive effect on Dena. The information seemed to free her; my half-sister had filed applications to go back to law school.

(Her houseguest, Katie, had mailed them for her. Then, on a rented bike, she had ridden away and never come back.)

I switched channels now. I stopped for a second at paid programming, which was Marthe's successful new infomercial. Then I hit the all-news channel, which had a brief mention of Troy Kevlin's latest indictment on drug charges. Finally, I lingered on the entertainment network, which featured news of the cancellation of Howie Romaine's new sitcom, *Romaine Land,* after just three episodes. Only I knew why these changes, good and bad, had taken place.

My last stop was the local news. There was coverage of a robbery at the Queens home of a police detective, Emile Florent. The lawman himself, looking flustered and bedraggled, was giving a reluctant interview.

"Only things of personal value were taken," he said, then turned away.

If I had been paying more attention, maybe I would have seen a crummy white Honda on the street where he and I had made our deal.

Bound to sell *Clown,* Stanley was on the loose again. Who knew what other treasures he would pursue? He wouldn't be contacting Abner again, that was for sure. My old pal had curtailed his ambitions to just running his Web site, back in his parents' house.

Then the phone rang. It was Jody. She wanted to know who played the peddler in *Macaroon Heart,* now unspooling on LCM. But, mostly, a little worried, she wanted to know where I'd been hiding myself.

"What have you been up to, Roy?"

I warned her that it was a long story. It was okay with her. Then, as I started to explain, my call waiting kicked in.

"Hold on," I said, and pressed the little lever.

"Will you hold for Jerry Lewis?" a voice said.

I had a terrible sense of anticipation. My heart began to pound. Was something beginning or had it reached a conclusion?

Still, there was so much to tell Jody.

I thought of Stanley Lager, who was a trivial man in the worst sense: someone who didn't know what was important.

Then I took a deep breath.

"Tell him," I said, "that I'll call him back."

ABOUT THE AUTHOR

LAURENCE KLAVAN won the Edgar Award for Best Original Paperback for *Mrs. White*, written under a pseudonym. He is also the author of *The Cutting Room*, another novel featuring Roy Milano. His work for the theater includes the librettos for *Bed and Sofa*, for which he received a Drama Desk nomination, and the acclaimed *Embarrassments*. He lives in New York City.